BASKET CASE

A GRAY WHALE INN NOVELLA

KAREN MACINERNEY

GRAY WHALE PRESS

1

"It's egg-decorating workshop day, isn't it?" my handsome husband John asked as I carried the last of the breakfast dishes from the dining room of the Gray Whale Inn. It was springtime in Maine, and although it was still a lot colder than I was used to for April (I'd grown up in Texas), the sky was bright blue, spring bulbs were unfurling their brightly colored blossoms, and the edges of the woodland outside the inn were sprinkled with wildflowers whose names I hadn't yet learned. On my walk the day before, I'd gathered purple hyacinth and a few narcissus for the vase on the windowsill above the sink, and I couldn't help but stop and sniff them every time I walked into the kitchen. Mixed with the comforting scent of the cinnamon-apple muffins I'd made for breakfast, the scent of spring flowers made the inn smell like something Martha Stewart would have happily bottled and sold for millions.

"Yes, the wax-pattern workshop is today!" I said, putting the dishes down and stopping to give Biscuit, our resident orange tabby, a few pets. She was in her favorite sunbeam spot on the floor near the radiator; her younger companion,

Smudge, was nowhere to be seen. Probably upstairs playing hide-and-seek with a catnip mouse, I decided as the patter of galloping paws sounded from overhead. I looked at the empty egg cartons on the counter from our preparations the day before. "I'm excited to learn how to do the wax-pattern decorating. Agnes helped me blow out a couple dozen eggs yesterday; that's why we had scrambled eggs for breakfast," I said.

"Win-win then," John said. "I love your scrambled eggs! And I talked with Agnes over breakfast; she seems lovely."

"She is," I agreed. Agnes Masaitis, whose parents had hailed from Lithuania and who had learned the traditional Easter craft from her own grandmother, had pitched the idea for an egg-decorating workshop to me months ago. Since I had some Lithuanian heritage, I'd been intrigued, and signed her up immediately. Although she lived in nearby Ellsworth, she'd had come to the Gray Whale Inn a day early to help me get everything ready for the workshop, which would be a mix of out-of-towners who had decided to make a weekend of it alongside a few locals. The workshop had been good for business; although it was a beautiful spring day outside, April in Maine could be unpredictable, and it was a hard time of year for bookings. "Will you put the rest of the dishes in the dishwasher while I put down some vinyl tablecloths in the dining room?" I asked.

"Of course!" John gave me a heart-stopping smile; even though we'd been together for a few years now, his sandy hair and green eyes still set my pulse racing. John was the island deputy and had grown up spending summers on the island before returning to pursue life as an artist. When I bought the Gray Whale Inn, he came as part of the package, as he rented the carriage house behind the gray-shingled former captain's house. We'd started as friends, but before long, we had fallen in love, and now we were partners in life... and innkeeping, which was a delightful side benefit. Many hands, after all, make if not light work, then at least lighter work. As he stood at the sink, I wrapped my arms around his flannel-clad chest and squeezed, inhaling a quick whiff of his woodsy scent. He turned and squeezed me back, then kissed me on the head.

"You're the best," I said, and fairly floated back into the dining room, almost forgetting the stack of tablecloths I'd gathered for the wax-pattern workshop.

As the door to the kitchen swung closed behind me, I heard voices from the parlor beyond.

"He never should have married you," I heard a woman hiss. "I told him, but he wouldn't listen."

"I'm glad he didn't listen. He loves me, and I love him!" a younger woman replied, anger in her voice. I sighed; I knew exactly who it was.

"You just want him for his money, don't you? Well, I wouldn't get excited about it. Before he died, Ralph and I made sure you'll never touch..."

2

~

"Anyone in here?" I called, hoping to interrupt them before words were said that couldn't be taken back. If it wasn't already too late.

"Natalie?" Mercedes, a young, dark-haired woman with a sweet, round face popped around the corner, her face flushed. A moment later, her mother-in-law appeared behind her, a brooding angry look on her sharp features, her gray-streaked brown hair pulled back into a severe bun. She reminded me of an angry nun. "Oh, I'm sorry," Mercedes continued. "We didn't realize anyone was here!"

"Just getting ready for the workshop," I said. "I'm really excited; Agnes came and helped me prepare the eggs yesterday, and I think it's going to be a treat.'

"Justine is an artist," Mercedes said, nodding toward her mother-in-law, who was still looking at her as if she were an unfortunate piece of forgotten Tupperware she'd found in the back of the fridge. "I'll bet her work will be amazing."

Justine sniffed. I had to give Mercedes points for effort. "What kind of dye is she using?"

"I don't know," I admitted. "I'm just providing the eggs and the venue; she's taking care of all the rest. She did say we should wear old clothes, though; I hope you brought something you don't mind getting color on!"

"Of course we did," Justine said condescendingly. "And remember, I'm allergic to peanuts, so no peanut oil or peanuts in any of the food you provide."

"I remember you telling me when you made the reservation," I said.

"Good. Now, if you'll excuse me, I'm going to meet my friends for our morning walk. I'll see you at the workshop." She turned and walked away; a moment later, as I unfolded the first tablecloth, I heard the front door open and close.

"Can I give you a hand with those?" Mercedes asked as I smoothed the tablecloth down.

"No need," I said. "That sounded rough; are you okay?"

She sighed. "I invited Justine to this to try to smooth things over with her," she said. "I'm afraid it seems to be backfiring."

"I saw that one of her friends is here, too."

"Two of them, in fact," she said. "Justine told them about it, and now it's the four of us. We went to that lobster pound on the dock last night and all my mother-in-law did was complain about Mary running for the school board and tell Phoebe she should make her HOA sue the people across the street from her for painting their house the wrong color."

"And she still has friends?"

"I know, right?" she said. "Seriously, though; let me help with that."

"Thanks," I said, handing her a tablecloth. Together, we

spread it over one of the tables by the window. "Do you and your husband live close to her?"

"We're all in Ellsworth, but Aidan and I are about a half hour away from his mom. Not nearly far enough, if you ask me." Her shoulders sagged. "I really hoped this weekend would help us connect find common ground, but all she talks about is money, and how I'm not going to get any. Like I married Aidan for his mother's money. It's so... hurtful." Her face flushed.

"I'm sorry," I said. My own mother-in-law lived in the carriage house behind the inn. We'd had a few rough moments, but had come to a point of mutual respect, and I was grateful for it. It was hard being enemies with your partner's parents. "She saves the best for you, eh?"

"She's kind of mean to everyone, actually. I'm realizing that today; I guess that makes me feel a little better."

"A little," I said. I was about to ask how her husband's relationship with his mother was when the door from the kitchen swung open and my very pregnant niece Gwen appeared.

"Hi, sweetheart!" I said, smiling at Gwen, whose pale face was surrounded by a halo of dark curly hair and whose tiny frame was dwarfed by her enormous baby bump. The baby was due any day, and half the island had already knitted the future addition blankets, booties, and hats. "Gwen, this is Mercedes. She and her mother-in-law are here for the egg-decorating class." I grinned. "You know a little about in-laws, don't you?"

"Mine are great, but my husband is a saint for putting up with my mother," she said, then looked at me. "You know she's coming when the baby's born, right?"

"I have a room reserved for her next week," I told her. Gwen's mother, my sister Bridget, had been less-than-thrilled to learn that her daughter was marrying a lobsterman and pursuing a career in art instead of finishing her degree and going into something sensible, like business. They had arrived at an uneasy detente, with "uneasy" being the operative word.

"When are you due?" Mercedes asked.

"Two weeks," she said, her hands resting on her pregnant stomach. "I don't know how I'm going to make it that long, though. I can barely sit down as it is!"

Mercedes had a hopeful look on her face. "What's it like, being pregnant?"

"Exciting. Terrifying. Heartburny." Gwen grinned. "Are you thinking about having kids?"

"We have," she said, with a glow that told me she was more than ready to start a family of her own. "That's part of the reason I invited my mother-in-law for this weekend. I guess I was hoping to make peace with her before we bring a child into the family."

"I hope it works out that way," Gwen said encouragingly. "I'm so glad to have my Aunt Nat around, even though my mother's far away. Family is good." My niece shot me a smile that warmed my heart.

"I'm sure we'll get the family thing figured out," Mercedes said with an attempt at a smile, then reached for another tablecloth. "Do you need any more help?" she asked me.

"Go relax," I said. "Looks like you'll have a full afternoon ahead of you; take some me time."

"Maybe I should," she said, and grinned. "And maybe another slice of cake?"

3

I followed my own advice once I got the tablecloths laid out, pulling on a pair of hiking boots, putting a bit of food into the cats' bowl, and stepping out into the spring morning. Biscuit and Smudge, who'd abandoned the catnip mice at the sound of the food bag rustling, dug in greedily as I closed the door behind me and headed down the path behind the inn. Gwen had gone down to John's workshop to ask his opinion on a new painting series she was considering starting, but had assured me she'd be back in time for the workshop. Based on the tension I'd experienced with Mercedes and Justine just a few minutes before, I was grateful.

The sun was high in an impossibly blue sky and the crisp air smelled of green and promise, and the path along the cliff beckoned. John was working on something in his workshop behind the inn; I could hear hammering through the open door as I walked toward the path leading up from the inn, breathing the cold sea air and feeling it fill my lungs. While we were at the workshop, John had told me he was planning on going to the town pier to deliver more of his toy boats to Island Artists and pick up a grocery order from the mainland. It was good to have help with the chores and errands that came with running a bed-and-breakfast. As I climbed the rise to the path, I turned back and looked at the inn, feeling pride swell in me at the sight of it.

The gray-shingled Cape Anne was nestled into the rocks and trees of the island, looking like it had sprung from the earth. Although the gardens were still dormant, I knew that in a few months, purple and pink lupines would cloak the sloping meadow that stretched down from the inn toward the rocky coast, and the bushes lining the path would be full of fuchsia beach roses with their deep, winey scent. Soon, I would be planting pansies and lobelias and geraniums in the window boxes again, and the inn would be full of summer vacationers, come to escape the craziness of life on the mainland.

I'd given up my own mainland life in Texas years ago, after a chance trip to Maine brought me to Cranberry Island and I had fallen in love with the gorgeous shingled Gray Whale Inn. On instinct, I had put an offer in on it, cashing out all my savings in a gamble that even now I was amazed I had the courage to take. I was so glad I had, though. Now, instead of living in a cubicle at the Texas Parks and Wildlife Department in Austin, I was the proprietor of the Gray Whale Inn, the wife to a sweet, gorgeous man, and part of a thriving island community full of people who had become dear friends.

Life can surprise you when you take chances. Sometimes in wonderful ways you never could have expected.

I took one last look at the inn that had been the home to so much of my life the last few years—and soon would see a new life, in the form of my grand-niece or nephew—and turned to head down the path, hopping over a few slushy mud puddles and pulling my jacket tight against the chilly wind off the water below.

I hadn't gone far when a trio of women appeared, Justine at their head, the same sour look on her face I'd seen earlier.

"Hello again," I called.

She grunted a response, and I stepped off the path into a patch of half-melted, icy snow to let her pass. And pass she did, with two equally dour looking women in her wake; I got the strong sense that something had happened among the women, one of which shot me a tight-lipped smile and the other simply a sharp nod.

"See you shortly!" I called as they tramped down the path toward the inn. I found myself hoping they took their shoes off, or at least wiped them off, before going inside. They were women, I remembered then; women were usually the most mindful of dirty shoes, since they seemed to be the ones who usually cleaned up after them. With Justine and her pals, though, I wasn't sure that would be the case.

Poor Mercedes. It was like putting a gourami in with a pack of piranhas. I made a mental note to see if Gwen would sit with her, to provide moral support; I had the feeling the young woman might need it.

I headed down the path a little further, and was about to turn back when a piece of paper caught on a tangle of branches caught my eye. It was a photograph that had been printed on a color printer. One corner was wet where it had made contact with a bit of melting snow, but it looked like it hadn't been there long enough for the ink to run. I picked it up; it showed a man and a woman embracing on a beach; I couldn't see her face, but from what I could see of his, I didn't recognize him. I looked back over my shoulder in the direction the three women had gone. Had one of them dropped it? I picked up the photo, folded it in half, and tucked it into my pocket. Then, after one last gaze out at the mountains on Mount Desert Island, their craggy pink granite slopes still frosted with snow despite the warmer weather, I turned back to the inn.

4

---

*A*gnes emerged from her room about a half hour before the workshop was scheduled to start, while I was refilling the coffee carafe and setting out milk and sugar for the workshop participants. She was a short, solid woman with a cap of steel-gray hair and intelligent eyes magnified by her thick glasses; I could sense both kindness and hurt in her, and I had the feeling she'd seen some serious challenges in her time on the planet. In addition to the basket of blown eggs we'd prepared the day before, Agnes had brought her supplies, and was laying out candles, little metal cups, pencils, pins, and sheets of sweet-smelling beeswax.

"Can I do anything for you?" I asked.

"Yes, actually," she said, her gray-blue eyes shining as she dug several boxes of dye out of her fabric bag. "I'll need some boiling water to make the dyes; could you put the kettle on? I brought vinegar."

"It's just like traditional Easter eggs!" I said.

"Almost," she said.

"How did you get started doing these, anyway?" I asked.

"My mother taught me," she said. "Her mother came from Lithuania when she was a young woman; making *margučiai* is one of the traditions she passed on." She pronounced it "margoochay." "The craft comes from centuries ago... decorated eggs were supposed to provide protection, and both the symbols and the colors had meaning. Flowers mean children, green is youth and growth, brown is the earth... I have a list you can use when you design your own eggs."

"It sounds amazing," I said, intrigued. "I can't wait to get started. Let me go get the water going!"

I headed into the kitchen to start some water boiling and fill a tray with goodies for the workshop. I'd baked some of my famous Wicked Blueberry Coffee Cake, of course, but also whipped up a batch of cranberry scones—without nuts because of Justine's allergy—she had demanded that I clear the inn of all nut-based products. I laid the scones all out on a pretty platter and walked them out to the buffet in the dining room as the kettle heated; by the time I had the platter set out and had augmented it with plates, napkins and forks from the cabinets in the sideboard, Justine and her posse had arrived, along with a very unhappy-looking Mercedes. Fortunately, Gwen walked in the back door at the same time; Mercedes lit up when she saw her.

I was glad to see the two young women situate themselves at a table near the window without my even having to ask Gwen to look out for the young woman. Mercedes appeared to have given up on appeasing her husband's mother, at least for the time being. As everyone settled into their chairs, Justine gave a start.

"I know you," she said, looking at Agnes.

"Yes, we've met," Agnes said coolly. "You're Justine Simonds. I'm Agnes Masaitis."

Justine blinked at Agnes, who looked to be in her seventies, whereas Justine was on the younger side of sixty. "How do you know me? Are you from the area?"

"I live in Ellsworth now," she said, "but I lived in western Pennsylvania most of my life."

"Hmm," Justine said, narrowing her eyes at her. "Windabay?"

"No," Agnes said with a small Mona Lisa smile.

"I can't place it."

"I'm sure it'll come to you." Agnes shrugged her round shoulders and continued pouring dye into the cups. As she reached for the vinegar jug, the kettle sounded from the kitchen.

"I'll be right back," I said, and hurried through the swinging doors into the kitchen to retrieve the kettle.

As I poured the hot water into the cups, two more people arrived: Emmeline Hoyle and Claudette White, both talented fiber artists and islanders I loved seeing. Emmeline was dressed in a hand-crocheted cardigan that clung to her round form, and Claudette's gray hair was pulled back into a severe bun, although her broomstick skirt hinted at a softer side—which was also apparent from the way she cared for her goats, Muffin and Pudge, who she cherished like children but who were the bane of the island's gardens.

"I brought some of my cardamom banana bread," Emmeline said, proffering a loaf wrapped in tinfoil, "but it looks like you've got the goodies taken care of."

"Are there nuts in it?" I asked.

"No, I'm afraid... I was out of walnuts, so I skipped it." Her bright brown eyes were sharp and sparkly as always, and I was glad she and Claudette would be joining the out-of-towners at the inn for the workshop.

"Thank goodness. I've got someone here who's allergic

to nuts... so I'll put some out," I said. "I love your banana bread; I make it all the time, but it never turns out as well as yours!"

"Anything sugar-free?" asked Claudette, who, despite swearing off sweets, somehow managed to maintain a rather solid figure.

"Of course," I said. "I've got some egg muffins set aside for you. Let me go put the kettle back in the kitchen and I'll get them... and a plate for the banana bread." More of the bed-and-breakfast guests filtered into the dining room as I scurried back to the kitchen again; it was a pair of mothers from a ritzy neighborhood in Ellsworth, a town on the mainland, who had decided to make it a weekend girls' trip and were staying at the inn. Kayla, a petite blonde with bobbed hair, stopped me on my way into the kitchen. "Any way we can have some mimosas?" she asked.

"I've got orange juice, but no chilled sparkling wine," I said.

"Oh, we've got sparkling wine in a cooler upstairs," she said. "I'll bring enough for everyone; we decided to get a case!"

"I'll bring the orange juice and some glasses, then," I said, adding both items to my mental list of things to retrieve.

"Wonderful," the younger woman said. "Mimosas it is!" she announced as I pushed through the door into the kitchen. It was shaping up to be an interesting afternoon, I reflected, and it hadn't even gotten started yet.

5

---

*D*espite Agnes's preparations, the workshop didn't get started until fifteen minutes after it was scheduled to begin. It had taken that much time to distribute glasses (everyone except Claudette and my pregnant niece had said 'yes' to mimosas) and get settled.

Pippa had taken the bottle of Prosecco and was doing the rounds of Justine's table with a bottle of Prosecco when she paused. "Kayla can't seem to get away from you, can she?" she said to the older woman.

"What?" Justine asked.

"You're Justine Simonds," she said.

"You're Pippa, right? You live in the neighborhood."

"I do. You're the one who caused all the trouble with Kayla," she said, nodding at her friend, who seemed uncharacteristically quiet.

"Excuse me?" Justine said.

"You're the one who reported our addition and got the HOA all riled up," Pippa said. "Thanks to you, she had to completely dismantle the deck addition she started." She turned to Kayla. "Can you believe she's here?"

"That's ancient history," Kayla said lightly, but her jaw was clenched. "Drop it, Pippa," she said in a warning voice.

Justine sniffed. "I didn't do anything to your friend; she was the one who didn't follow the rules. We make rules to be followed," she said. "People who don't follow rules have to pay the price, don't they?" she asked, shooting a meaningful glance at Kayla, who looked away, cheeks burning.

What exactly was Justine talking about? I felt like I was missing something.

"You cost my friend and her husband tens of thousands," Pippa said. "I shouldn't give you Prosecco. I'm only doing it because I'm a nice person." She filled Justine's glass, then did the rounds of the rest of the table before plonking the bottle down and stalking back to Kayla's table. Kayla put her hand on her friend's and whispered something into her ear. Pippa shot another narrowed-eye glance at Justine and then took a sip of Prosecco, crossing her arms.

"May I have your attention, everyone?" Agnes began from the front of the room. "I am Agnes Masaitis, and I want to thank you all so much for coming to learn how to decorate eggs the way I learned as a child from my parents and grandparents. Today, we're going to learn to make *margučiai* just like my grandmother did." She went on to describe the two traditional techniques—one involved applying wax and then dipping the eggs, whereas the other involved dipping the eggs, then scratching designs into them with a sharp implement. As she spoke, I scanned the room. Justine had given up on orange juice and was drinking the Prosecco straight up... and making what seemed to be a concerted effort to pretend Kayla didn't exist.

"Today we will be using beeswax," Agnes continued from the front of the room. "If you are making these in the Russian style, you use something called a *kiskas*, which is a little metal funnel, but the way we do it is to use a pin. Let me demonstrate," she said. As we watched, she stuck a pin into the eraser at the end of a pencil, then dipped the pin head in a little cup of melted beeswax suspended in a small metal stand over a candle. "Now you just apply the wax in the way you want to start your design," she said, and as we watched, she created a beautiful vining pattern around a white blown egg. "Once you are done," she said, "you can dip the egg in the dye—it's a little tricky, since it's hollow, so you have to be gentle—and either add more wax before dipping it again, or let it dry and remove the wax with a hot towel." I'd agreed to toss some old towels in the dryer at the end of the workshop so we could reveal everyone's designs. She put down the egg she was working on and pulled a box out of her bag, lifting the lid to show a half-dozen gorgeously decorated eggs in a rainbow of colors, covered with spirals, leaves, wheat seeds, stars and suns.

"Come, take a closer look," she invited everyone. Slowly, the women left their tables and approached the box of beautifully decorated eggs.

"These are amazing!" Kayla breathed. Agnes smiled, then looked at Gwen, who appeared enthralled. "You might want to put some flowers on yours," she suggested. "They mean children."

Gwen blushed and touched her hand to her swollen belly. "I will," she said. "But it won't look anything like these, I'll bet."

Agnes laughed. "Give it time. I've been doing this for fifty years, after all. Now. If you are all ready to get started, I have sheets with the traditional designs printed on them, along with colors, and what each one means." Everyone bustled back to their tables, and I could sense excitement as Agnes distributed the blown eggs and the pages with the list of symbols and colors on them. A few women headed back to examine the samples Agnes had brought with her before embarking on their own designs, but Justine and her two friends launched right in.

"I'm going to use the deer for wealth and prosperity," Justine announced.

"Might want to use a few circles for protection, too," her friend Phoebe said with a slight sneer. She was almost surgically thin, with a long, aquiline nose that seemed designed for staring down, and like Justine, she wore tailored slacks, a windbreaker, and fancy walking shoes that looked like they probably cost more than my monthly mortgage payment.

"You do like to make enemies, don't you?" her other friend commented. Mary, I remembered her name was, from when I'd checked her in. She had a more human build, with a jeans and cozy wool sweater that looked like it had come from the Aran Islands and a smile that was genuine... unlike Phoebe and Justine, she seemed like someone I'd enjoy getting to know.

"I just speak my mind," Justine said.

Mary snorted.

I was sitting with Emmeline and Claudette, contemplating my own egg and deciding what I wanted to attempt.

"I don't see goats on this sheet," Claudette said.

"Probably because they'd eat all the flowers," Emmeline joked, giving her friend a nudge.

"True," Claudette acknowledged. Her two goats, Muffin and Pudge, were the bane of the island's flower gardens. "I'm going to do one anyway. Or try to. Maybe I'll make a Muffin and Pudge egg!"

"What are you going to do, Natalie?" Emmeline asked. She was already busy dipping her pin in beeswax to create a design of stars and spirals that reminded me of a galaxy.

"I don't know yet," I said, consulting the sheet of paper. "Maybe leaves for life and growth..."

"A flower for children," Emmeline added.

"Of course," I said, glancing over at Gwen, who was in deep conversation with Mercedes as she applied wax to her egg with short, deft strokes.

"Is it a girl, or a boy?" Claudette asked.

"I don't know yet," I said, looking over at my friend. She had been forced to give up her own child in more repressive times; as a young woman, she'd been what at the time they called an 'unwed mother,' and had given up her baby for adoption at birth. Fortunately, she'd reconnected with her lost child just a few years back, and was now a proud grandmother whose adorable grandchildren were frequent visitors to the island. I knew she was thrilled to have reconnected, but the pain of the lost years of motherhood was still there. "It'll be interesting being a great-aunt," I said. "I've never had children of my own, and when Gwen was growing up, she was with my sister in California, so we didn't see each other much."

"It's an adventure," Emmeline said. "She and Adam had better sleep while they can; babies never let you catch a wink."

"You and John still have time," Claudette said. "Have you ever thought about it?"

"Not seriously," I said, suddenly feeling anxious as I attempted to create a leaf shape that looked like the one on Agnes's sheet using the pin head dipped in wax. It was not going well. "I guess we'll see how it goes with Gwen."

"It would be fun for two little ones to grow up together," Emmeline said. "And we could use more youngsters on Cranberry Island."

"Easy, now," I said. "I've got plenty on my plate as it is.

I'm not sure John and I are ready to add parenthood to the mix."

"I'll bet Catherine would love it," Emmeline said. My mother-in-law Catherine was currently in Boston visiting friends, and I found myself thankful she wasn't here to join the chorus.

"What color are you thinking of dyeing your egg, Emmeline?" I asked, looking for a way to change the subject.

"I'm going to do a deep blue," she said, "maybe with a bit of purple."

As she said the word "purple," there was a crash from across the dining room.

6

—————

"*J*ustine!"

Mercedes raced over to where her mother-in-law lay on the floor, clutching at the pink scarf around her neck. Justine's face was red, and her eyes bulged.

"Is there a doctor here?" Mercedes asked wildly, looking around the dining room. Everyone was frozen, staring in horror as she hurriedly untied the scarf. "I think it's anaphylaxis. Her purse. I need her purse."

I jolted into action, hurrying across the room and retrieving the voluminous canvas bag slung over the back of Justine's chair. "What do you need?" I asked.

"There should be an EpiPen in there somewhere," she said. "It's orange and yellow." I dug through the bag for a moment, sifting through the debris that accumulates in any large purse, then dumped the contents on the floor, scattering them in search of something yellow and orange.

"It's not here," I said.

"Check her room," Mercedes said. "And somebody call 911!" Everyone in the room fumbled for their phone as I stood up. Justine's wheezing had intensified, and her face was almost purple now; it was horrible to look at. I raced out of the dining room and through the entryway, then down the hall to the Lupine Room, where I knew Justine was staying. The door was locked. I sprinted back down the hallway to the front desk, grabbed the skeleton key from the bottom drawer, and raced back down the hallway.

Justine's suitcase sat next to the door, neatly zipped. I tore it open, but it was empty. I hurtled into the bathroom and threw open the drawers and cabinets, then searched her dresser drawers before finally pulling open the night stand drawer and finding a plastic cylinder labeled "EpiPen". I grabbed it and raced back to the dining room, where I handed it to Mercedes.

She opened the plastic cylinder and pulled out the injector, then jammed it into Justine's leg, right through her cotton pant leg. Justine's wheezing had gone ominously silent.

"Please, God, please, God, let it work," Mercedes prayed out loud. I echoed her in my head; I hadn't liked Justine from what I knew of her, but I didn't want her to die, either. We all watched and waited, hoping she would start breathing again.

"Is there anything else we can do?" Phoebe asked timidly.

"I don't think so," Mercedes said. "We just have to wait and hope it works."

"I'm calling 911," Gwen said. She grabbed her phone and dialed; a moment later, a dispatcher answered. Gwen told her what had happened, and a moment later relayed to us we'd done everything right and that they were sending the paramedics our way. "She wants me to stay on the line," Gwen said, cradling her stomach with her free hand as if that could somehow protect the baby from the awful scene in my dining room.

I nodded, thanking her.

"What caused this?" Agnes asked.

"An allergic reaction," Mercedes said, then looked at me. "Were there peanuts in any of the baked goods?"

"No," I said.

"I don't put peanuts in my banana bread," Emmeline added.

"Peanut oil, maybe? Or peanut butter? It doesn't take much at all to cause a reaction," Mercedes said.

"No," Emmeline and I responded. I looked at the plate next to Justine's chair, praying that nothing I'd done had resulted in the poor woman lying on the dining room floor. There were the remains of a piece of blueberry coffee cake and an untouched slice of banana bread, and her coffee cup was half-full of black coffee.

I looked at her wine glass, and noticed something in the bottom of it.

"What's this?" I asked, lifting it into the light and wondering if maybe she'd dropped a crumb of coffee cake into the glass by mistake. Then, with dawning horror, I realized that it wasn't a crumb in the bottom of the glass.

It was a chunk of peanut.

I put the glass down hurriedly and stepped away, as if I'd just handled a smoking gun. Which, in a way, I guess I had.

"There's a piece of peanut in her glass."

Mercedes's head whipped up. "How did it get there?"

"I don't know," I said. "It's just a piece of peanut; is that enough to cause this kind of reaction?"

"It takes almost nothing with a peanut allergy," Mercedes said. "Are you sure there wasn't one in the glass when you set the table?"

"We store them upside-down, so I know it was empty when I put it on the table. And I don't have any peanuts or peanut products in the kitchen; I made sure to get rid of them when I found out Justine had an allergy."

"It got there somehow," Mercedes said, looking around the room and pausing at Kayla.

Kayla's eyes widened. "Don't look at me," she said. "I didn't bring anything downstairs. Besides, I don't eat peanuts unless it's an emergency. Too many lectins."

Her friend Pippa looked confused, and she turned to Kayla. "What are lectins?"

"It's just... you want to limit them," Kayla said.

I had no idea what lectins were, but I didn't feel like pursuing the issue just now . "Anyone else have a peanut in their glass?" I asked. "Or see any peanuts anywhere?"

Everyone searched their tables and their glasses, but the rest just appeared to contain Prosecco and orange juice.

"I need another cup of coffee," Emmeline announced, walking over to the buffet table and grabbing a mug. As she poured a cup of coffee, her hand shook a little bit, sloshing a bit of dark liquid on the table. "I'm so sorry, Natalie," she said. "I shake a little when I'm upset."

"Don't worry about it," I said, heading over to the buffet table and grabbing a napkin. I mopped up the spill and went to throw the soiled napkin into the trash, then sucked in my breath. Half-hidden by crumpled napkins was the top of a blue plastic bag labeled MIXED NUTS.

7

"Who had mixed nuts?" I asked, looking around the room.

"I... I had some in my room," Pippa said. "But I didn't bring them down."

"There's a bag in the trash," I said.

"Are there peanuts in it?" Mercedes asked from next to Justine's prone form.

"There are," I said, without needing to look at the label; I recognized the bag, and knew peanuts were the main ingredient. "Is she still with us?" I asked.

"Her heart is beating, but I'm afraid we're going to lose her soon. Are you sure there's not an EpiPen in her purse? You're supposed do a second dose if the first doesn't work. She always carries one."

We pawed through her bag again, but there was no sign of an EpiPen. Mercedes squinted out the window toward the blue water. "How long does it take emergency services to get here, anyway?"

"Depends on whether they come by helicopter or boat," I said, "but either way, it's not as fast as I'd like."

"I'll ask," Gwen said, but the dispatcher couldn't give an answer.

"I don't think they're going to get here as fast as Justine needs," Mercedes said, slumping against the wall. "This was such a terrible idea," she said. "Why did I invite her here?"

"You were trying to build a bridge," Justine's friend Phoebe said kindly. Beside her, Justine's other friend Mary nodded; for the first time since I'd met them, I saw softness in their eyes as they looked at Justine's daughter-in-law, who was wiping tears from her own eyes.

The sound of a boat engine thrummed outside a moment later. I looked outside to see a Coast Guard boat heading toward the Gray Whale Inn's dock, but I was afraid it was too late.

"She's not breathing," Mercedes said.

"The paramedics are here," I reassured her. "I'll go meet them."

John emerged from his workshop as I pushed through the back door of the inn. He looked down at the dock, shading his eyes from the sun. "What's going on?"

"One of the guests had an allergic reaction," I explained, and he joined me as I hurried down to the dock. John helped them tie up as the paramedics leaped off the boat and followed me up the path to the inn.

"She's allergic to peanuts and had a reaction," I said. "She's not breathing."

"Do you have an EpiPen?"

"We gave her one injection," I said.

"How long ago?"

"Ten minutes," I estimated.

"We'll give her another one," he said.

The dining room quickly became a hive of activity as the EMTs went to work. They administered another EpiPen shot, then set to work trying to revive her. Mercedes watched, hand to her mouth, tears streaming down her face, while the rest of us gathered around the edge of the room, not sure what to do. I looked down at the case of beautifully decorated eggs. It seemed like days ago that we'd been admiring the beautiful colors and designs.

"Oh, Justine," Mercedes moaned. "I'm so, so sorry this happened."

Phoebe wen̶   ̶he younger woman and put her arm around her. "It's okay," she said. "It's not your fault."

"It is my fault," she said. "If I hadn't invited her here..."

"It's not your fault," Phoebe said firmly.

"Poor thing," Agnes murmured, looking at Justine; she'd materialized at my side at some point during the proceedings. "She seems like a very unhappy person."

"She is," Phoebe confirmed from my other side, where she was still comforting Mercedes. "We're friends, but I must admit, she's always been quick to find fault and thought everyone was out to get her."

"How did you meet Justine?" I asked, well aware that someone in this room had put that peanut into Justine's glass... and wondering why Phoebe was friends with someone she'd just admitted was unlikeable.

"We're all on the Windabay Homeowners' Association," Phoebe said. "We're not very popular in the neighborhood, as you can imagine," she said, glancing toward Kayla, "so we just kind of stick together."

"What was Justine talking about, with Kayla following the rules?" I asked, looking at the younger woman, who was clustered with her own posse near the windows.

"Justine is in with the architectural committee," Phoebe said. "New people keep moving into Windabay and trying to change things, often without asking. Justine doesn't like change."

"Including a new daughter-in-law, I gather." Mercedes had drifted over toward Justine again, and had put her cell phone to her ear, no doubt calling her husband to tell him the news.

"Aidan is her only son, and nobody on this planet would ever be good enough for him," Mary said, rolling her eyes. "Poor Mercedes. Aidan really is in love with her, and I can see why; she is very sweet, even if Justine doesn't see it."

I looked over at Justine, whose face was contorted in a horrible way. "How is she?" I asked the EMT who was doing chest compressions.

"She's still not breathing," the EMT said, winded from the effort of trying to revive her. "We're going to keep working on her while we take her in."

"Can I go with her?" Mercedes asked.

"Are you family?"

"She's my mother-in-law," Mercedes said.

"Come along, then," he said, and Mercedes headed out to the dock as the rest of us looked on. I watched the young woman follow her mother-in-law's stretcher, her head bowed. My heart hurt for her; it was so sad that a weekend that was supposed to be about healing had turned out to be anything but.

8

---

*a*gnes continued the workshop after the coast guard left, but the mood in the room was somber, and Justine's empty chair was like an accusing eye. I had given my phone number to Mercedes to let us know how Justine was doing, but hadn't heard anything yet, and had a bad feeling. What should I do about the police? I'd told the EMTs that Justine was allergic to peanuts and that there'd been a piece in her drink, but they had been so focused on keeping Justine alive they hadn't said anything about the police.

We had all finished decorating our eggs and were about to dye them John came in through the back door.

I looked up, relieved to see him, then pushed my chair back and stood up. Without speaking, we both walked into the kitchen; I was relieved when the door to the dining room swung shut behind me.

"Did the paramedics have anyone come out to talk to the women at the workshop?" he asked when I told him I'd found a peanut at the bottom of Justine's glass... and a nut bag in the trash can.

"No," I said. "And then I just kind of tried to make everything as normal as possible, considering one of the women was hauled out on a stretcher."

"Any word from Mercedes on how she's doing?" he asked.

"Not yet," I said. As I spoke, my phone vibrated in my pocket. It was a Maine number I didn't recognize, and I felt myself tense up as I answered.

It was Mercedes, from the hospital.

"She's gone," she said in a hoarse voice. "She didn't make it." She stifled a sob. "How am I going to tell my husband?"

"We'll deal with that later," I said, looking at John and shaking my head. He rubbed his chin and then reached for his own phone as I talked to Mercedes. "Did you tell the folks at the hospital that we found a peanut in her glass?"

"Not that it was in her glass, just that she had a peanut allergy. They tried everything... it just happened too fast." She sobbed. "I just realized. I don't even know... I need somewhere to stay tonight.. how do I get back to the inn?"

"The mail boat runs regularly," I said. "Or John and I can take a skiff to the mainland and pick you up in the car we keep on the mainland, if you're coming back later. Whichever feels better."

"I think I'd rather take the boat," she said. "I think I need a little time alone. To process."

"Okay," I said. "But let me know if you change your mind. And we're here if you need anything at all."

"Thanks," she said. "I... I guess I'd better call Aidan."

"Why don't you wait till you get back," I said. "We can keep you company."

"Would you?"

"Of course," I said.

"All right, I guess." She sounded like a little girl.

"We'll be down to meet you at the next mail boat unless you change your mind. I'll keep my phone on," I told her.

"Thanks, Natalie."

"Of course," I said. "And I'm so sorry."

As I hung up, I could tell John was talking with the mainland police. He was the island deputy, and now that Justine was gone, we likely had a murder on our hands.

"They're on their way," he said when he hung up a moment later.

"Lovely," I said. "At least everybody who's not from the island's staying at the inn... but this isn't exactly the kind of community relations I wanted from this weekend."

"We'll get through it," he said, walking over and giving me a big, woodsy-scented hug. "Is the workshop over?"

"No," I said. "We're about to dye the eggs."

"Why don't you go finish up, take your mind off things."

I snorted. "Right."

"It's better than sitting in here stewing," he pointed out, and I had to agree with him.

I slipped back into the dining room just as everyone was finishing dyeing their eggs. I didn't want to disturb everyone with the bad news just yet. But as it turned out, I didn't really have a choice.

"How is she?" Agnes asked, interrupting her talk of dyeing methods.

"Mercedes called a moment ago. She didn't make it," I said.

There was a collective intake of breath. "Oh, Justine," Mary said. "She always said she'd end up choking on a peanut one day, but I never expected it to actually happen." Her face, along with Phoebe's, was grim. "She was such a force of nature; it's hard to believe she's gone."

"Poor woman," Agnes said, in a voice oddly devoid of emotion. Then again, she had just met Justine.

Or had she? I remembered Justine's certainty that she and Agnes had met. I eyed the instructor through a new lens; had she had something to do with what had happened to Justine?

"Who here knew she was allergic to peanuts?" Emmeline asked, her dark eyes bright as always.

"Well, we did, of course," Phoebe and Mary said.

"And I did," I said. "She made no secret of it; I cleared the kitchen of peanut products before she arrived. She was very careful. It's a shame Pippa didn't know."

Agnes spoke from the front of the room before we could say anything else. "You can either be finished here, or if you'd like to add a layer of pattern, you can put another set of designs on with wax and then dye them again," she said.

Everyone decided that was the way to go, but the eggs needed to dry first. As I gazed at the list of suggested designs, wondering what to add next, I decided it would be best not to let anyone know the police were coming just yet.

I checked my egg, which had turned a lovely spring green, and decided on a floral pattern for my next addition. As we waited for the eggs to finish drying so we could decorate them further, Phoebe said to Agnes, "Justine said she knew you, but I can't figure out how."

"Maybe we ran into each other in Ellsworth," Agnes said with a slight shrug.

"Where do you live, again?"

"Near the center of town," Agnes said. "In an old house. You?"

"We're in one of the newer subdivisions," Phoebe said.

"The gated one?" Agnes asked.

"Windabay? Yes," Phoebe said. "You know it?"

"I remember when they were rezoning that area," she said. "There used to be a farm I liked to go to." She gave Phoebe a sad smile. "All the beautiful places are just eaten up by big houses these days, aren't they?"

Phoebe stiffened. "We bring value to the area," she said. "Windabay has done a lot for property values."

"And taxes," Agnes said. "Many of my neighbors are having to leave their homes; they can't afford to stay."

"I'm sure they made plenty of money when they sold," Phoebe said.

"Yes, but where will they go?" Agnes said sadly. "My neighborhood is becoming short-term rentals. Soon, I'll be the only long-term resident on my street."

"That's why we forbid those in Windabay," Phoebe said in a self-righteous tone.

"Didn't Justine try to talk you into going in with her to buy a few houses?" Mary asked Phoebe. "Just a year or two ago? For summer rentals?"

"I don't remember," Phoebe said, looking away unconvincingly. "Anyway," she said. "We should probably finish up here. I think I need to go lie down."

"Yes," Agnes said, looking at me. "It may be time for the hot towels so we can finish."

"I think we need to stay here," I said.

Kayla's brow furrowed. "Why?"

"The police are coming to ask us a few questions," I informed them.

Phoebe grimaced. "Why would the police be involved? It was clearly an accident, what happened."

"It's just a formality," I said, not entirely truthfully.

"Hmm," Emmeline said; as usual, she'd been watching everything with her sharp eyes. "Well, then. Maybe I'll put another set of designs on mine. It'll help pass the time, anyway."

"So we're under house arrest?" Kayla asked, pulling her chin back and looking down her nose at me.

"I wouldn't put it that way," I said. "Like I said, it's just a formality."

"I should have brought more Prosecco," Kayla said,

upending the bottle over her glass and taking a swig. She and her friends began conferring in low, agitated voices.

"Let's finish the workshop up while we're waiting," I said, hoping to get everyone doing something with their hands. I turned to Agnes. "Is this dry enough to work with?" I asked, pointing to my green egg.

"It is," she said. "I have to be back to pick up my dogs this evening. Will they be done before the last mail boat, do you think?"

"If worse comes to worst, we can take you over to the mainland in one of our skiffs," I offered.

"Oh. Okay," she said, but she didn't look like it was okay.

"I promise we'll get you back," I said. "Now... what should I do with this egg?" I asked, making yet another effort to get everyone's mind off what had happened a little while ago. I thought again about the mixed nuts bag in the trash... and looked around the room, wondering who had slipped that peanut into Justine's drink.

And why.

10

"That was one heck of a day," John said when we finally sat down at the kitchen table together hours later.

"I know," I said, leaning back in my chair in the kitchen and petting Biscuit, who had jumped up into my lap. My buttery yellow kitchen was warm and comforting after the day's events; while John put together a plate of cheese and cold cuts for us, I'd made a batch of chocolate muffins and popped them into the oven, where they were now perfuming the air with a comforting chocolatey scent. The sun was almost down over Mount Desert Island, and a few last shafts of light gilded the rounded mountains and made the trees outside take on a golden hue. I took a sip of the sauvignon blanc John had poured for us and stabbed a piece of cheddar. "I'm so glad everyone decided to go out for dinner; baking is therapeutic, but I really didn't want to cook a meal."

"I would have taken care of it," John assured me.

"You're the best," I said, reaching across the table and squeezing his hand.

"How's Gwen doing?" Ever since she'd announced her pregnancy, John had been very protective of her, and concerned for the baby's health. It made me wonder if he might want children of his own... something we probably needed to revisit. But not today.

"She was upset, of course, but she seemed okay. She and Adam are going to come over for dinner tomorrow," I said.

"It's hard to believe that in two weeks, we're going to have a new niece or nephew."

"I know," I said, feeling a warm glow that was welcome after the trauma of Justine's death. I kept thinking about her falling to the floor, and her labored breathing. I shuddered a little at the memory of her face as she struggled for oxygen. "What's the take from the detective?" I asked.

"I don't know that she's made a determination yet," he replied, but I could tell by the furrow between his sandy eyebrows that he was concerned that what had happened that afternoon in the dining room was no accident. "I'll call tomorrow morning for an update. How's Mercedes doing?"

"She's shaken, of course," I said. I'd picked her up from the mail boat a few hours ago and sat with her while she shared the news with her husband, Aidan, who was still in California. He was on his way to the inn and would be here the next day; in the meantime, Phoebe and Mary had taken over keeping Mercedes company, whisking her off to Spurrell's Lobster Pound for dinner. "I would be, too. I just keep thinking it can't have been an accident. Justine was absolutely adamant about peanuts... she didn't want me to even have any in the inn. And her daughter-in-law said she kept an EpiPen with her at all times, but it wasn't in her bag."

"There was one in her room, though," John pointed out

as he reached for a little roll of prosciutto. "Maybe she just forgot it."

"Maybe," I said. "But she was so persnickety that doesn't feel right."

"You think maybe someone put a peanut in her glass and took the EpiPen?" he asked, turning his wine glass in his hand. "And is one peanut really enough to kill someone?"

"I looked it up; peanut allergies can be really brutal. Even if you have a bite of something with peanut butter in it and spit it out, it can still be fatal."

"That's crazy," he said.

"I know." I was very grateful I didn't have to contend with life-threatening allergies... particularly living on an island with limited access to medical facilities.

"All right," John said. "I'll bite. Who do you think would have wanted to kill Justine?"

"I really don't know if anyone would have had an adequate motive for murder, to be honest. At least not one I'm aware of. On the other hand, I did just meet Justine, and we weren't best friends or anything."

"What *do* you know?"

"Well, she didn't like Mercedes. She made it very clear that she thought she wasn't good enough for her son... and she wasn't shy about making sure Mercedes knew it."

"Ouch," John said.

"I know," I agreed. "And it turns out Justine was on Kayla's homeowners' association and cost Kayla a lot of money by putting a stop to her construction project."

"So that's two people who weren't enamored of Justine," John said. "But neither seems like a likely candidate for murdering her." He took another sip of wine. "She came with friends. Do you think maybe there was something going on with one of them that we don't know about?"

"It's possible," I said. Then I remembered the picture I'd found on the trail that morning. I dug it out of my back pocket once again and unfolded it. "What do you think of this?" I asked, smoothing it out on the scarred pine table and pushing it over to him

"What is it?" he asked.

"I found it on the cliff path," I said. "In the wake of Justine, Phoebe, and Mary, who looked like they'd just argued about something."

"Who are they?" he asked, peering at the picture again myself. It was a zoomed-in shot of a fit-looking couple in a passionate embrace on a beach. Although the woman's face was obscured by her hair and the man's hand, a diamond tennis bracelet adorned her slender wrist, and her manicured fingers sported what appeared to be a large sapphire ring on her third finger. He had light blond hair and a deep receding hairline, and appeared to be about six inches taller than her.

"That's the question," I said. "I think it might have something to do with what happened. But it doesn't look like this woman is any of the women here at the inn."

"Do you know it came from them?"

"No," I admitted. "Maybe I'm grasping at straws." I took a sip of my wine; as I put down the glass, John pointed out the window behind me. "Is that Mercedes?"

I turned to see the young woman trudging down the hill. "It is," I said. "I thought she was with Phoebe and Mary!"

"She isn't now," John said. I stood up and headed to the front door of the inn to meet her. She was just starting up the path to the porch when I opened the door, letting a blast of cool, fresh spring air into the inn.

"Hey," I said. "Are you okay?"

"No," Mercedes said. "I'm not okay. I can't find Justine's phone, I just had to tell my husband his mother died, and now I feel horrible I invited her here in the first place. Nothing's okay." And then she burst into tears.

11

"Come on in," I said, hurrying down and putting my arm around her. "John and I were having a glass of wine in the kitchen; do you want to join us?"

She hesitated, then said, "Maybe one small glass. It'll help me sleep."

"Come on, then," I said, leading her through the dining room, past the place where Justine had had her allergic reaction, to the swinging door that led to my warm, butter-colored kitchen.

"Hey," John said as we entered. "Let me get you a glass."

As I led Mercedes to a chair, John grabbed a glass from a cabinet and poured a bit of wine into it, setting in front of her. "You've had quite a day," he said.

"It just keeps getting better," she said.

"What happened?"

"Phoebe kind of suggested that I was the one who killed Justine," she said, and swiped at her eyes. "She asked if Aidan and I were going to move into her house, now that it's going to be ours, and whether I'd planned this trip just so I could do it in a place that would deflect suspicion." She took a ragged breath. "She says she's going to tell the police her suspicions."

"What did Mary say?" I asked.

"She didn't say anything at all," Mercedes said. "They're vipers, the two of them. All three of them were... sorry, that's horrible of me. Forget I said that."

John and I glanced at each other. A moment later, Mercedes caught sight of the picture on the table. "What's this?"

"We were just wondering that," I said.

"Natalie found it on the path this morning," John said. "It might be nothing, but it's possible it had something to do with what happened to your mother-in-law. Do you know either of these people?"

Mercedes picked up the paper and squinted at it. "No, I don't recognize them," she said. "Although you can't really see any of the woman's face, can you?" She put it down and looked at John. "Why do you think this might have something to do with what happened to Justine?"

"Justine, Phoebe, and Mary had just walked by the spot where Nat found it," he said. "We were wondering if maybe one of them dropped it accidentally."

Mercedes shook her head. "I have no idea who these people are."

"Mercedes said she can't find Justine's phone," I told John.

"Are you thinking maybe somebody 'disappeared' it when she had that reaction?" He asked.

"Maybe," I said. "I just thought it was odd."

"We should keep looking for it, but I agree." He turned to Mercedes. "Would Phoebe or Mary have any reason to want Justine out of the way?" he asked.

She blinked. "You think one of Justine's friends might have killed her?"

"If Phoebe's trying to tell the police that you did it, maybe she's covering her tracks," I suggested.

"Oh. I hadn't thought of that," she said. "I can't think why they would. They were all tight... they liked to sit around and judge everyone else all the time."

"Did they judge each other?"

"I feel like people like Justine judge everyone all the time. It's like a reflex."

"Was there anyone else who was angry at Justine? Or have a reason to want her gone?"

Mercedes shook her head. "Not that I know of. In fact, the only person who really benefits from her death is my husband." Her shoulders sagged. "Which is what Phoebe said tonight, about six times. I couldn't take it anymore; I had to leave the table."

"I'd leave, too," I said. "After the day you had. That must have been just horrifying."

"It was," she said in a small voice. "Justine and I never got along, but she was my husband's mother. If it weren't for her..." She sobbed and put a hand over her stomach. "Actually, part of the reason I brought her here was to share some good news. Aidan and I are pregnant."

"Congratulations!" I said.

"And I never got to tell her. And now the baby will never get to meet his or her grandmother." Tears rolled down her cheeks anew, and I reached over and squeezed her shoulder.

"I am so sorry," I said. "Are you close with your own mother?"

Mercedes nodded. "She's going to be thrilled. She's coming for a visit next week, and I was going to tell her then."

"When are you due?"

"September," she said with a small smile. "It'll be a fall baby. We don't know if it's a boy or a girl... we decided to wait and find out."

"Gwen and her husband Adam made the same decision," John said.

"She told me," Mercedes said. "We were dyeing eggs together; she's lovely."

"She is," I said, smiling at the thought of my kind, talented niece. Who was going to be a mother any day now.

"I... I think I need to go lie down," Mercedes said.

"Of course," I told her. "We're here if you need us, though. And I'm sure you could reach out to Gwen, too. Do you have her number?"

"I do," she said, standing up. "Thank you so much. I needed this." She took a deep, shaky breath. "I can't wait for Aidan to get here."

"When will he arrive?"

"He's in California for a work conference, but when I told him... he was just quiet for a long time." A groove appeared between her eyebrows. "He'll be on the first flight tomorrow morning. He should be here by early afternoon."

"How did he take it?"

"He was... stoic," she said. "But I know it shook him up. He's lost both parents now."

"Thank goodness he's got you," I said.

"I just hope Phoebe doesn't manage to convince the police that I'm the reason she died," Mercedes said, then gave us a small smile. "Thanks so much for everything. Really." And then she disappeared through the swinging door.

12

---

*A*s the door swung closed, I took a sip of wine and looked at John across the pine kitchen table. Biscuit jumped up into my lap and began kneading my legs; I petted her absently, wincing a little bit at the claws poking through my denim jeans.

The wind was picking up outside, and I could hear the sighing of the pines out the window; it was almost like they were trying to tell me something I couldn't quite make out. The egg I had decorated that morning was next to the vase of hyacinth and narcissus; although it had turned out beautifully, with a delicate tracery of leaves and flowers, just looking at it made me think of Justine. Had someone wanted her dead? Or was what had happened just a crazy accident? "I keep thinking about that half-empty bag of mixed nuts in the garbage can in the dining room," I told John, taking a sip of my wine. "Nobody admitted to it being theirs."

"Would you?" he asked. "Given the circumstances?"

"It would be awkward," I admitted. "I'd feel horribly

guilty if I'd somehow accidentally been responsible for someone going into anaphylactic shock. Although how a peanut ended up in Justine's drink is a real mystery."

"I know. How could that possibly happen by accident?" John asked.

"Exactly. It's not like there were peanuts on the table, or anything. Or anywhere, for that matter. She made sure I cleared the inn before she got here."

"Maybe one of her friends forgot and accidentally sent one flying when they opened the bag?"

"Justine would have said something if someone turned up with nuts. Besides, Phoebe knew Justine had a peanut allergy," I mused. "I'm sure Mary knew, too. That could point to one of them being the culprit." I turned my glass around in my hand, admiring the glow of the straw-colored liquid. "On the other hand, it was hardly a state secret; she told everyone at the beginning of the workshop that she had a peanut allergy."

"Why would Phoebe want Justine dead?" John asked, spearing a chunk of white cheddar with a toothpick.

"I wondered the same thing. I'm thinking whoever opened that bag of nuts probably left prints, though."

"That's why I stashed the garbage bag in the laundry room earlier in case the police decided they needed evidence," John reminded me.

"You did? That's quick thinking. Does anyone who was in the dining room see you take it?"

"I don't think so," he said, shaking his head. "I just kind of tied it up and walked into the kitchen with it while everyone was talking about Justine."

"But I did announce to everyone in the room that I'd found it."

"So if there was a killer, they would have been watching. And if they knew we'd kept the bag, they'd be keen to get rid of it," John said. "Maybe I should put it up in our closet, just to make sure. I'll be right back," he said, standing up and heading into the laundry room, giving my shoulder a squeeze on the way.

A moment later, he appeared at the laundry room door with the bag in his hands.

"It's gone," he said.

"What's gone?"

"The bag of mixed nuts. It was in here when I tied it up and put it in the laundry room, and now it's not." His handsome face looked grim. "Which means what happened to Justine was no accident. "I'll have to tell the mainland police about this."

"Maybe whoever it was left fingerprints on the garbage bag," I suggested.

"Good point," he said. "I should have used gloves."

"Your prints would be on the bag anyway," I reminded him.

"Who's the deputy here, anyway?" he asked, grinning. "You're right, of course, but I may have obscured other prints." He sighed. "This is looking a whole lot more like it wasn't an accident. I'm going to put this up in our room and lock the door until I can get it to the investigators."

As he headed up the stairs to our private quarters, trash bag in hand, I took another sip of wine and looked out the window. The beam of a flashlight was bouncing down the driveway toward the inn; Phoebe and Mary must be returning from dinner at the lobster pound.

"They're coming back!" I called.

"Why don't you meet them in the parlor?" he called back

down the stairs. "See if you can get them to stay for a glass of wine. Maybe they'll tell us something useful."

"I'm on my way," I said. "As long as you promise to join me." I was guessing the presence of my handsome husband might loosen tongues more than just having me on the sofa.

"I'll be there in a minute," he promised.

13

A gust of cold air whooshed into the inn along with Phoebe and Mary, whose cheeks were flushed from the walk back from the town pier. I had positioned myself on the sofa in the parlor along with a fresh bottle of wine and my glass.

"Hi, ladies! How was it?" I asked.

"It was delicious," Mary said. "And the lemon fool for dessert was to die for."

"They do a good job, don't they? They used to be closed all spring; I'm glad they started opening up earlier. Can I interest you in a glass of wine? John and I were about to start a fire in the fireplace," I said, feeling inspired.

The two women looked at each other and then shrugged. "Why not?" Phoebe said.

"Pull up a chair and I'll grab some glasses," I said. As they settled themselves on the sofa across from mine, I walked to the kitchen and retrieved John's glass along with two fresh ones from the cabinet.

I was about to push back through the swinging door when John came back downstairs.

"Are they in?"

"They are," I confirmed. "But I promised them a fire in the fireplace."

"You're better at that than I am," he said, "so I'll pour the wine."

Together, we returned to the parlor, where the two women were discussing something in low voices. At the sight of us, they stopped talking abruptly.

"Ooh, thank you," Mary said as I set down two fresh wine glasses. John twisted the top off the bottle of Sauvignon blanc and poured them each a dollop as I busied myself arranging logs in the fireplace and tucking crumpled back issues of the *Daily Mail* in between the logs. Soon, flames licked the wood, and with a bit of coaxing and a couple of rounds with the bellows, a cozy fire crackled away, filling the parlor with warmth and heat.

I returned to the sofa and settled in next to John, who put his arm around me.

"How are you two holding up?" I asked as they each sipped their wine.

"It was a shock, of course," Phoebe said.

"Do you think it was an accident?" John asked, surprising me a little with his directness.

"What else would it be?" Phoebe answered, shrugging, but her eyes narrowed.

"Who stood to benefit from her death?" I asked, although Mercedes had already told me that her husband was in line to inherit.

"Oh, Mercedes and Aidan, of course."

"I heard Justine telling her the other day that the will was set up so that Mercedes wouldn't inherit anything," I said.

"I wouldn't know about that," Phoebe said. "But if Aidan inherits, then they both benefit, it seems to me."

"Do you think Mercedes might have slipped a peanut into her mother-in-law's drink?" John asked. "Nat tells me there was some tension between the two women."

"Just normal mother-in-law-daughter-in-law stuff," Phoebe said, waving the idea away. "I'm sure Mercedes had nothing to do with what happened."

"It was an accident anyway," Mary said.

"I don't know what they're ruling it," John said, taking another sip from his wine and pulling me a bit closer.

Mary blinked at him. "They'll let us go home, though, right?"

"You live on the mainland," John said. "Ellsworth, right?"

She nodded.

"You live in the same neighborhood as Kayla, don't you?" I asked.

"Yes. Now, there's one who wasn't too happy with Justine," Mary said.

"Because of the construction ban, right?"

Phoebe nodded. "It cost Kayla and her husband about thirty thousand dollars."

"But it's a nice neighborhood, isn't it? I mean, thirty thousand dollars isn't a life-and-death amount in Windabay, is it? I remember going on a homes tour a few years ago; if I remember right, those are million-dollar houses."

"It's an affluent neighborhood, yes," Phoebe allowed. "But that's still a lot of money."

"Did you know Kayla well?" I asked.

Phoebe sniffed. "We weren't really friends, no. Acquaintances, but that's all." She sighed. "I wish Mercedes hadn't put up that workshop notice in the community area. Maybe this wouldn't have happened."

"So that's why so many people at the workshop come from Windabay," I said. "I wondered why! Oh, by the way, I wanted to show you two something."

"What?" Phoebe asked.

"A photo I found the other day," I said, as John's eyebrows rose. "It's in the kitchen; I'll go get it."

I hurried into the kitchen and retrieved the printed-out photo I'd found on the path, then walked back to the cozy parlor and handed it to Phoebe, watching her face. She looked at it with genuine curiosity; I saw no sign of alarm from either her or Mary.

"Do you recognize either of them?"

Phoebe shook her head. "It's kind of hard to tell, though; you can't see much of their faces, can you?'

"No," Mary agreed, squinting at the photo and shaking her head. "Where did you find this?"

"On the trail," I said. "This morning; I wondered if maybe Justine showed it to you, and then accidentally dropped it."

Phoebe shook her head. "She didn't show it to us. Maybe it's a coincidence, and it came from someone else."

"Maybe," I said, looking down at the photo of the embracing couple. Were they somehow connected to what had happened to Justine?

Or was I just grasping at straws?

14

The next morning was, predictably, a complete 180 from the previous day's bright sunshine and (relatively) warm ocean breezes. Another front had come through during the night, and cold rain lashed the kitchen window panes as I whipped up the batter for a lemon sunshine Bundt cake; I figured we could all use a little sunshine this morning, considering the circumstances.

The coffee brewed, filling the kitchen with the welcome scent of French Roast as I grabbed a few lemons from the refrigerator and pulled a zester out of the drawer. By the time I'd finished zesting two lemons, adding a zingy citrus aroma to the already delicious-smelling air, the coffee had finished, and I poured myself a cup, doctoring it with sugar and a good dollop of milk before adding the zest to the butter I'd creamed a few minutes ago, along with some sugar.

I was about to start cracking eggs into a bowl when my phone rang. It was Gwen. My heart jumped as I picked up the phone; any word from Gwen before ten was more than likely an emergency.

"Are you okay?" I asked as I picked up the phone.

"I am," she said, "but I've started having contractions."

I leaned up against the counter and, for one of the first times ever, wished we didn't live in a place that made trips to medical facilities harder than they could be. "Is Adam with you?"

"He is," she said. "The thing is, I'm not due for another two weeks, and everyone tells me first babies are late."

"I wish I had more experience," I said, feeling helpless. "I just don't know."

"Well," she continued, "the contractions aren't regular, and they're still quite a ways apart. That probably means it's not real labor, but I just don't know. I've never done this before."

"I haven't either," I said. "What does your mother say?"

"I don't know; it's way too early on the west coast. Besides, if I call her now..."

"She'll be on the first plane from California today, I know," I said. Adam and Gwen had told me they didn't want my sister Bridget to come until after the baby had arrived, but if Bridget knew her grandbaby was on the way, there was no way we were going to be able to hold her off.

"When is the midwife's office open?" I asked.

"Eight-thirty," she said.

I glanced up at the clock. "An hour and a half. Maybe Adam should take you over so you can see her first thing?"

"It's raining cats and dogs out there," she said. "Besides, we were hoping to have the midwife come and do a home birth."

"Call her and ask," I said.

"This early?"

"She's a midwife," I reminded her. "Babies come at all hours. I'm sure there's someone on call."

"You're right," Gwen said. "I'm just not thinking straight."

"You're eight and a half months pregnant," I reminded her. "I think that comes with the territory. Will you call me back and tell me what she says?"

"Of course," Gwen told me. "Thanks for the advice."

"I wish I had more," I said, and hung up, trying to remember where I was before Gwen called. I checked the recipe and looked at the bowl. Sugar. Putting sugar in the bowl. Had I put one cup in? Or two? I eyeballed it and guessed only one, hoping I was right as I turned the mixer on, and then went about cracking eggs into a second bowl.

I was going to have a grand-niece or grand-nephew soon. I knew that labor was incredibly safe these days, but I was still worried, both for Gwen and for the baby. And excited. What would it be like to have a baby? Did I want a baby? Was it too late for John and me to have a baby?

And why was I thinking about this when I had a potential murderer in the inn, a new family member on the way, and a lemon cake that was going to be an absolute disaster if I didn't pay better attention?

I somehow managed to get the cake into the oven and pulled the rest of the eggs we'd "blown" out of their shells from the fridge to make another batch of scrambled eggs. I was planning on cooking up some bacon as well, and maybe adding a bit of cheese to shake things up a little. I might put some of the bacon aside for a batch of potato cheese soup for Gwen and Adam... I could bring it over later on when I knew what was going on. Even if Gwen was in labor and couldn't eat yet, at least Adam would have something, and it kept well...

But that was later. Now, I had breakfast and guests to think about. Agnes was setting up for the second day of the workshop, and John had told me yesterday evening that the police were planning to come back and ask a few more questions.

I shuddered at the memory of Justine turning red and gasping for breath. Had someone killed her? And if so, who?

15

I wasn't too surprised to see several women with dark circles under their eyes waiting for me when I pushed through the swinging doors at 8:00 with a carafe of coffee in one hand and a cake plate of fresh Sunshine Lemon Bundt cake in the other. I did a mental headcount almost involuntarily, relieved that we weren't short anyone.

"You're here early!" I said, and Agnes grimaced at me.

"Is there coffee in there?" Kayla asked, squinting at the carafe.

"Please say yes," her friend Pippa added.

"Lots of it, and more brewing," I assured her. "Let me just put the cake down and I'll fill you right up. There's sugar on the tables, and I'll be out with half and half in a minute," I said. Kayla walked up to the table to be first in line for coffee, holding out a slender hand with a coffee cup in it. She wore a diamond bracelet that winked in the morning light, and my thoughts turned to the bracelet in the photo I'd found. Was the photo of Kayla? She sipped her coffee ("black, unless you have heavy cream," she'd said, then announced, "I'm doing keto, so no cake for me, unfortunately"), and I studied her hand; instead of a sapphire ring like the one in the photo, she wore a slender gold wedding band. And in any case, her hair was honey-colored, not red like the woman in the photo.

Once I'd filled everyone's cups, I left them (well, everyone but Kayla) to the cake and hurried to the kitchen to refill the carafe and retrieve the half and half. By the time I got back to the dining room, the ladies had made quite a dent in the cake. "I've got scrambled cheesy eggs, bacon, and berry salad coming, too," I announced. "Save some room!"

As I bustled back and forth from the kitchen to the dining room, laden with coffee and fruit salad, I could sense the caffeine start hitting as the conversation grew into an animated hum.

"I still can't believe she died of a peanut allergy," Phoebe was saying as I refilled her coffee. "She was always so careful."

"It doesn't make any sense at all, does it?" Mary answered, shaking her head.

A moment later, at the other table, Kayla's friend Pippa was talking about the house construction. "Do you think you can bring the project before the HOA board again? Maybe they'll approve it if Justine isn't there."

"It's too early to think about that," Kayla said. "It just happened yesterday. Besides, we're thinking about selling. Jeremy has always wanted to build a house, and he has a line on a waterfront lot on Mount Desert Island…"

"You're leaving Windabay and moving to MDI?" Pippa asked, looking hurt.

"It's only a few miles away! We'll see each other all the time. Promise."

"You couldn't pay me to live on MDI, with all that

summer traffic," Pippa said. "Besides, what about the schools?" As they discussed the relative educational merits of Mount Desert Island and Ellsworth, I drifted away to check on Agnes, who was sitting by herself staring out the window.

"Thanks for doing the workshop... and for offering to put everything out today so the participants can dye more eggs. I'm so sorry this happened in the middle of everything."

Agnes gave me a small smile and sipped her coffee. "Thank you for having me," she said. "I've been meaning to tell you that I noticed that mixed nut bag too," she said. "I think I saw someone with it, or a bag like it."

"Who?" I asked.

"That's the thing. I just can't remember." She looked up at me with sharp blue-gray eyes. "Maybe they have more in their room," she suggested.

"I'll suggest it to the police," I told her. John had warned me too many times about snooping in rooms. On the other hand, I did need to go tidy. And as long as I didn't go opening any drawers...

"That would be a good idea," Agnes said, nodding.

I lingered for a moment. "Are you sure you didn't know Justine?"

She shook her head. "I think I would remember," she said simply, but her eyes flicked to the side. I nodded and topped off her coffee, then retreated to the kitchen, where John was finishing up the bacon.

"How goes it in there?" he asked.

"No dead bodies yet," I said, "so I'll take it as a win. Would you mind taking the bacon and eggs out? I want to look something up."

"Sure," he said. "The eggs are in the oven?"

"I finished them a few minutes ago," I said.

"What are you researching?"

I glanced up at him. "Agnes Masaitis," I said. "I think she knew Justine and she's lying. She told me she thought she saw someone else with a mixed nut bag, but I'm not convinced."

On a hunch, I flipped open my laptop and sat down at the kitchen table. I pulled up Google and typed in "Agnes Masaitis Justine Simonds."

There were ten hits on the first page. None of them involved Justine's name, but The first was an article from an Ellsworth community paper. "Masaitis Leads Anti-development Push Near Wildlife Refuge."

"John," I said. "There's a connection."

"What?"

"Agnes Masaitis was heading up an organization to block a project Justine's husband was involved in pushing through," I said.

"You're kidding me," he said, walking over to look at the screen.

"This article is from last year. She was trying to protect the waterfront area and get the city to turn it into a park."

"Did she win?"

"I don't think so," I said. "The council approved the development six months ago."

"Then what's Justine doing here at the workshop?" John asked.

"Mercedes signed her up for it," I said. "I don't know if Justine had any idea Agnes was the one going after her husband's development."

"But Agnes knew of her, I'll bet."

"Simonds isn't the most common last name," I agreed.

"But if it's already gone through, why kill Justine? Besides, it was her husband's company."

"He passed recently, didn't he?" John asked.

"I gathered that from a conversation I overheard. Let me check." I found Justine's husband's name—Ralph—from one of the articles and Googled it alone. Sure enough, his obituary appeared just three months earlier.

"That's interesting," John said. "Do you think Agnes might have been responsible for his death, too?"

The thought gave me chills. "You mean she got her revenge by killing both of them?"

16

"It's an idea," he said.

"But how would she know that Justine was coming to the workshop?"

"I sent her a list of participants. And it's not that hard to bring a bag of mixed nuts."

"Assuming she knew of Justine's nut allergy," he said.

"We could always check her room," I suggested.

He gave me a stern look.

"I mean while cleaning. If we see anything."

"No snooping," he said. "In any case, whoever had that bag of nuts wouldn't keep more of them around, would they?"

"You're probably right."

"Still, it couldn't hurt. I'll tell you what; why don't I clean with you after breakfast?"

"You sure?"

"If that's the only way I can keep an eye on you," he said, grinning.

"When are the mainland detectives supposed to be here?"

"At 11," he said, "so we should head upstairs early. If we see something, we can take a picture of it..."

"And then maybe they can get a warrant," I finished for him.

"Exactly," he said.

"Well, let's see if we can get through breakfast without a body and we'll see what we can find," I said.

BREAKFAST WAS A RELATIVELY QUIET AFFAIR. Once John and I cleared the plates away (most of my Bundt cake had disappeared), Agnes started the second round of the workshop; today we were going to learn the "scratch" method of egg-patterning. As everyone retrieved eggs from the basket for the second session and Agnes passed out a new set of handouts with instructions, I excused myself. Feeling some regret that I was only going to have wax-patterned eggs, I joined John in the downstairs hallway with a bucket of cleaning supplies in hand and we began with the first room.

Which was Agnes's.

"All right," I said, once the door closed behind me. "You want the bed, or the bathroom?"

"I'll do the bathroom," John said. As he headed into the bathroom, I surveyed the bed, which was already neatly made, and then ran a duster over the night stands. There was a King James Bible on the one next to the window, along with a pair of reading glasses. I checked to make sure John was out of sight before sliding the drawer open, but it was empty. Same with the other side. I then checked the dresser, which had a bottle of hand lotion and a hairbrush. A quick check of the drawers revealed nothing but clothes, and the trash was equally uninspiring, consisting of a few tissues and a piece of dental floss. I looked under the bed and even ran my hand under the mattress, but found nothing. The wardrobe was my last hope, but it contained only a few empty hangers, a windbreaker, and an empty navy-blue overnight bag. "Anything?" I asked once I'd run the duster over everything and plumped up the pillows.

"Nope," he said. "Just a bottle of shampoo and a few bobby pins."

"I don't know if I'm relieved or frustrated," I said. "I don't want it to be Agnes. But I do want to know who put that nut in Justine's glass."

"Shall we check the next room?" John suggested.

"I think so," I said, and a moment later we walked into what had been Justine's room until just yesterday.

"Let's not touch anything, just in case it is a crime scene," John said.

"Got it." Since I was with the island deputy, I felt a little better about letting myself into a guest's room. Besides, the guest was no longer around to complain.

I didn't need to unlock the door; when I turned the knob, it opened right up.

"She didn't lock it," I said.

"Or someone found the skeleton key and broke in," he suggested. "We should probably keep that somewhere a little more hidden than the front desk."

"You're probably right," I said as we stepped into the room, which looked like it had been hit by a tornado. The bedding was rumpled, the pillows were on the floor, and the drawers were all ajar.

"Someone beat us to it," John said.

"I think you're right," I agreed, scanning the room. I came to rest at the outlet next to the desk. "There's a laptop cord here," I told him, pointing to the outlet, and then to the empty desktop. "But no laptop."

"There's a canvas bag by the door," he said. "Let's take a peek." He put on a rubber glove and nudged the bag open. "Nothing but a windbreaker," he said. We did a scan of the rest of the room, but found no sign of a computer. "Did you ever see her using one?" he asked.

I shook my head. "But she was only here for a day, and it wasn't a work thing. Do you think someone took it?"

"That's my guess," John said. "Unless it was in the bag she took downstairs?"

"I dug through it looking for the EpiPen," I told him. "No laptop."

"Then where is it?"

"One of the other bedrooms?" I suggested. "We know it's an Apple, at least, based on the charger."

"Let's go, then," he said.

We worked our way through the rest of the downstairs, but found no Apple laptops or anything out-of-the-ordinary... until we stopped in Pippa's room.

On her night table, next to a book on The Keto Diet, was a six-pack of mixed nut bags. Two were missing.

"Well?" I asked, pointing it out to John.

"They're just like the bag you found in the dining room. Take a picture of it," he said. "She's certainly not hiding them."

"I know; she mentioned she had them when we asked. Do you think maybe it really was an accident? Or that she's got some secret reason for wanting to kill Justine?"

"I have no idea," I said, "but I plan to find out."

he workshop participants were just about to take their break by the time John and I finished up and walked through the dining room on the way to the kitchen. Emmeline and Claudette had arrived after breakfast, and were snuggled into a table by the windows. Everyone was busy scratching white patterns into dyed eggs, and as I looked at the stunning colors and intricate designs, I felt another twinge that I'd missed the rest of the workshop.

"I'll refill the coffee carafe and grab some snacks," I promised as I headed into the kitchen.

"I'll help," Emmeline offered, following John and me through the swinging door to the kitchen. Claudette followed her.

"Is there any fruit?" Claudette asked as I retrieved what was left of the Bundt cake and began filling the coffeemaker.

"I've got some bananas and apples," I offered. "And maybe a few grapes."

"That will work," she said, and picked up the printed photo on the table. "What's this?"

"It's a picture I found on the trail yesterday," I said. "After Phoebe, Mary, and Justine were out walking. I was wondering if it might have something to do with what happened to Justine yesterday."

"Who are these people?" Emmeline asked, standing next to Claudette and eyeing the photo curiously.

"I don't know," I said. "I wondered if the woman might not be Kayla, since she's got a diamond tennis bracelet on like the one Kayla's wearing. But Kayla's hair isn't red and she doesn't have a ring like that one."

Emmeline blinked at me. "She does. Have a ring. She was showing us her wedding photo earlier today." Emmeline peered at the photo. "It looks a whole lot like that one."

"But the hair is different," I pointed out.

"Not in the wedding photo she showed me," Emmeline said.

"And her husband has black hair," Claudette said. "Not blond, like this man."

Interesting. But not conclusive. "Maybe that photo was from before she was married?"

"Not before she was engaged, anyway," Emmeline said. "That ring was an engagement ring."

I looked at John, and he pointed to the woman in the picture. "So if that's Kayla, who's the man she's kissing?"

"I'm guessing if it isn't her husband, she might not want him to see this picture," I suggested.

"And you found it on the path right after Phoebe, Justine and Mary passed," John said.

I nodded. "I'm wondering if Justine showed this picture to Kayla. It would explain what she really meant about 'not following rules' the other day... and why Kayla didn't pursue it, even though Pippa wanted to. "

"So Justine tried to blackmail her?" Emmeline asked.

"Or threatened to tell her husband, if not blackmail her. That sounds like a valid reason for Kayla to put a peanut in Justine's drink," Claudette suggested.

"You didn't see anything, did you?" I asked.

"No," Emmeline said, "but Kayla was the one pouring Prosecco, as I recall."

"Perfect opportunity for her to pop something into Justine's glass."

As Claudette spoke, John's phone rang. He picked it up and listened for a moment, then walked toward the back window and looked out toward the lighthouse in the distance; I could see him grimacing as he listened. "Thanks for letting me know. Yes, check-out is tomorrow at 11; everyone should be here till then. Any results back from the autopsy yet?"

He was quiet for a moment, then said, "Are we treating this as an accident? Most people at the retreat knew she had a nut allergy." Silence for a moment, then, "Okay. We'll talk tomorrow, then."

"They're not coming today?" I asked as he hung up.

He shook his head. "They're short-staffed. They promised they'd be here tomorrow morning."

"So we have another night with a likely murderer in the inn," I said, then turned to Claudette and Emmeline. "Please don't tell anyone I said that."

"Like Gertrude at the *Daily Mail*, you mean?" Emmeline suggested.

"I'm surprised I haven't heard from her yet, actually," I said, then pulled out my phone. "Oh. Wait. My ringer's been off; she's called twice. And so has Gwen." In all the excitement, I'd forgotten to check in with my niece.

"Call her now," John suggested, but I'd already hit the "call back" button and was listening to the phone ring.

Gwen's husband Adam answered.

"How is she?" I asked. "I'm so sorry I missed her call!"

"No worries!" he said. "Contractions are still coming, but not regularly enough to qualify as active labor. The midwife's husband has a skiff; she's on alert. As soon as they get regular, she'll head our way."

"Can I talk to her?"

"She's in the bathtub at the moment," he said, "but when she gets out I'll have her call."

"Is she doing okay? Are you?"

"We're fine," he said.

"I'm making some potato soup for you guys," I said. "I know Gwen loves it."

"Gwen's not the only one," he said. "Thanks."

"Of course. Call me if there's any update, okay?"

"You're first on the list," he promised, then added, "Just don't mention that to Gwen's mom."

I laughed. "Of course not. We're here if you need anything at all," I reiterated, and hung up a moment later.

"She okay?" John asked.

"Not in full labor yet," I said, "but I have a feeling that's about to change."

"It's so exciting!" Claudette said, eyes sparkling. I knew she hadn't been able to raise her son, but she was making up for lost time with her grandchildren, who were the light of her life. "You'll love having a little one around, Natalie. Ever since the grandkids started visiting, it's changed my life. And they'll be here on the island... do you know if it's a boy or a girl yet?"

"It'll be a surprise for all of us," I said. "Now... we should probably get that coffee back into the dining room."

Emmeline glanced down at the picture on the kitchen

table. "What are you going to do about that?" she asked, jabbing a finger at it.

"I don't know yet," I said.

"Maybe give it to the detective tomorrow?" John suggested dryly.

"Maybe," I said, tucking it back into my pocket for safe-keeping.

But I wasn't promising anything.

18

I did join the workshop for the next hour, but my mind was on anything but the purple egg I was scratching leaf patterns into. Mercedes had gone to the airport to pick up her husband, Gwen was at home timing contractions, and Justine was... well, no longer with us, so it was a much smaller group today.

Instead of sitting with Emmeline and Claudette, I decided to sit down with Kayla and her posse, who were busy discussing houses. They'd popped another bottle of Prosecco and appeared to be most of the way through it.

"Windabay is nice," one was saying as I pulled up a chair at the table, "but I'm jealous that you're going to get to build on the water."

"It's a long-term dream," Kayla said. "We really decided to go for it when we had trouble with the HOA restrictions. We want the freedom to do what we want, you know?"

"What do the kids think?"

"They're excited," Kayla said.

"How old are they, again?" her friend asked.

"Seven and nine," Kayla replied. "They'll be at the same

school, so that won't change. And they'll just have to come visit!"

"You're so lucky," Pippa sighed. "Handsome husband, gorgeous kids, and now a waterfront house…"

"Sounds magical," I said. "Do you have a pic of the family?"

"I do!" she said, and pulled up her phone. "We just had these portraits done a few months ago." She showed me a picture of a beautiful family: Kayla, looking like she'd just come out of a salon, with a handsome, dark-haired man and two tow-headed children who would have been right at home in a Pottery Barn Kids catalog.

"Gorgeous!" I said, peering at Kayla's hand in the picture. "May I?" I asked.

"Sure," she said, handing me her phone. I zoomed in on the photo, examining her left hand. Sure enough, there was the familiar diamond tennis bracelet… and a ring with a large blue stone. "What kind of ring is that?" I asked, pointing to the photo. "It looks really unique."

"It's a sapphire," she said, puffing up a little bit. "Unfortunately, it's at the jeweler's right now; I lost one of the little diamonds flanking it."

"It's a stunner," Pippa said. "Almost the same color as her eyes."

Kayla fluffed up her hair and smiled, looking like the cat who had caught the canary. "Curtis bought it for me because my birth stone is sapphire."

"He's so amazing," Pippa cooed. It sure did look like Kayla was queen, and her friends ladies-in-waiting.

"I'm so lucky, right?" Kayla preened.

"Your husband's in the construction business, isn't he?" I asked.

"I guess you could say that. He owns a development

company," she said. "He's got a few neighborhoods he's building... one on Mount Desert Island, and a few more on the coast just across the bridge."

"He specializes in high-end houses," her friend piped up. "My husband, Jacob, works for the firm as an architect."

"And I help with interiors," Kayla said proudly, etching a line of dots into her hot-pink egg with a pin.

"It sounds like it's quite a family business," I said.

"It is, actually. Curtis's father started it, and he's just taken the helm in the past year or two. Building things runs in the family... I'm hoping my kids will step into the business when we're ready to retire."

"That's great; it sounds like your family's really close. How long have you and Curtis married?"

"Coming up on ten years now," she said. "I can't believe it. I don't feel old enough to have been married ten years!"

"Time flies, doesn't it?" I mused, scratching a very freeform leaf into my egg. "It must have been frustrating to have to deal with the HOA restrictions at Windabay. How much did you end up losing?"

Kayla's smile faltered a bit, and her eyes darted to me. "Oh, not that much," she said.

"Not that much? Kayla, Justine cost you tens of thousands of dollars!" Pippa said, and then swallowed when she realized what she'd said. "Of course," she amended hurriedly, "that's a drop in the bucket for your family."

"It was a lesson learned," Kayla said.

"A tough one," I said, scratching another leaf into my egg. "I think I'm going to get another piece of cake. Anyone else want one?"

"Oh, I'm on keto," Pippa said. "Which is a real shame, because lemon cake is my favorite."

"I know, right?" said Kayla. "I miss carbs."

"No carbs?" I asked. "What do you eat?"

"Oh, you know. Meat, cheese. Salad. Lots of salad."

"I'm not sure I could manage that," I said. "But good for you!"

"Can you believe she forgot to bring snacks?" Pippa said. "She usually has beef jerky with her, but I had to slip her a bag of nuts for a snack yesterday, before the workshop. But she didn't eat any of them down here... just in the room.". She shot a worried glance at her friend.

"Look at that design you're doing!" Kayla said hurriedly, pointing to the Pippa's egg. "Is that a dragon?"

"Did you talk with Justine at all once you got here?" I asked Kayla. "It must have been kind of weird, since I know you weren't on friendly terms."

"No," Kayla said quickly.

"Yes you did," Pippa said. "Remember? You told me you ran into her when you were on your way downstairs to get an extra towel."

"Only for a moment," Kayla said. "You know, maybe I will have a piece of that cake," she said, getting up. "Anyone else?"

"I have another bag of nuts upstairs if you want," Pippa offered.

"I'm good," she said, shooting her a look that would have probably felled me.

"When did she have those nuts yesterday?" I asked.

"Before breakfast," she said, and then her eyes widened. "Are you thinking Kayla was the one..."

"How are your eggs going?" Agnes interrupted, coming over to check on our designs. Mine looked like it had gotten into an unfortunate altercation with a fully clawed cat, but I simply smiled and told her it was going great.

"Oh, how pretty," she said, admiring Pippa's much more

expert effort. "And this one is lovely, too," she added, indicating Kayla's raspberry-sherbet colored egg, which featured a spiral of intricate designs.

"Thanks," Kayla said; she'd returned with a small slice of cake. "I realized why you seemed familiar," she said, glancing at Agnes. "Weren't you the one who was really involved with protesting the development Justine's husband was pushing forward?"

Agnes stiffened, and her smile looked suddenly wooden. "We had our differences of opinion."

"But you and Justine got along?" Kayla pressed. "How did you know she was going to be here, anyway?"

"I didn't until I saw the sign-up sheet," Agnes said. "Why are you asking me this?"

"Because I think you're the one who put that peanut in Justine's drink," Kayla said.

*a*gnes blanched. "What? Why would I do that?"

"Because her husband's company beat you out and got your special coastline developed."

"I would never do something like that!" Agnes replied, her back stiffening and her chin tucking in. "I am a God-fearing woman. I would never commit murder."

"Kayla," I said. "I found this on the trail after Justine and her friends walked down it yesterday morning." I pulled out the photo I had tucked in my back pocket and flattened it on the table.

A flash of fear crossed Kayla's petite features, and she blinked hard before recovering herself. "What's that?" she asked. She swung a hand, and her coffee cup spilled, the dark liquid covering the two figures in the picture.

I grabbed a napkin and mopped up the spill before it could soak into the page and looked at Kayla, who had gone pale. "I was going to ask you that. That looks like your bracelet."

"Maybe, but that woman's hair's red," she said, reaching

to grab the picture. I pulled it away before she could snatch it from the table. "Mine is blonde."

"Your hair was red last year," her friend Pippa said, as I handed her the picture. Kayla looked almost physically sick as Pippa pointed to the ring on the woman's finger. "And that's your ring. Who is that with you?" She peered at the picture and then pulled back, looking at Kayla in horror. "That's Jacob. Oh my God, Kayla. What are you doing kissing my husband?"

"It's not what it looks like," Kayla protested. "I don't know where this picture came from. It must have been photoshopped."

"Oh my God," Pippa repeated. "This is Mussel Quay. Jacob goes running there all the time. I recognize his running shorts. You were having an affair with my husband all this time?"

"No!" Kayla said. "It was... just a hug."

"That's not a hug," Pippa said, her voice cracking. "I thought he might be seeing someone. I just never dreamed it would be one of my best friends." Tears leaked from her eyes. "How could you do this to me? How could Jacob do this to me? Both of you. Oh, God..." Pippa crumpled into the nearest chair.

"It's not what it looks like," Kayla said, talking fast and blinking. "It was nothing."

Pippa swiped at her tear-streaked cheeks, looking up at her friend. Her voice shook as she spoke. "Nothing? Sleeping with my husband didn't mean anything?"

"It's just a made-up photo," Kayla said in a weak voice, but she wouldn't meet Pippa's eyes.

"It's not, though. Justine threatened you with it," I said.

"She was just trying to keep my husband and me from

suing the HOA," Kayla said. "It's not real. It doesn't mean anything."

"You put a nut in her drink when you were pouring the Prosecco yesterday," I said. "I found a bag of mixed nuts in the trash, and your friend here says she gave you a pack yesterday morning because you needed a snack."

"I... You have no proof," she said. "This is all conjecture."

"I know you were sleeping with him," Pippa said. "That is no made-up photo. And you weren't hugging. You were kissing." She peered at the photo. "And his hand is on your... oh, God." She ran out of the dining room, sobbing. Kayla sat very still in her chair, as if by not moving, she would somehow disappear. She reminded me of a cornered animal; all her fight was gone.

"I still have the mixed-nut bag I found in the trash," I said quietly. "It's the same brand that Pippa brought to the retreat, and I'll bet we find your prints on it. What did you do with Justine's computer?"

"I think I have the answer to that," John said. He'd come into the dining room without my noticing, and was holding a bashed-looking laptop in a gloved hand. "I found this on the rocks about fifty feet from the dock when I went down to bail out the skiffs. I'll give it to the detectives when they come; you may not know this, but salt water takes days to degrade fingerprints."

"All right," Kayla said, shoulders slumping. "I put a peanut in her drink. But I meant it as a warning. She was threatening to send this photo to my husband, and if she did that..." Kayla straightened her shoulders. "Everything would be ruined. I couldn't let her do that."

"So you killed her and tried to destroy the evidence."

"I couldn't find that damned photo," she said. "But I

figured it was on her computer. If I could get rid of that, maybe nobody would find the printed copy..."

"And her phone?"

She nodded.

"Where is it?" John asked.

"In the water. I threw it in with the computer." She swallowed and looked up at John, widening her eyes. "I didn't mean to kill her. I just meant to... to scare her."

"Is that why you stole her EpiPen?" John asked, pulling a yellow pen-shaped injector in a plastic bag out of his pocket.

"Where did you find that?"

"On the beach," he said. "Near the laptop. I'll bet we'll find your prints on this, too."

"It was a mistake," she said. "I didn't expect her to die. Please. I can explain it..."

"You can explain it to the detectives," John said. "They'll be here in less than an hour. In the meantime, you have the right to remain silent..."

"No!" She said, and ran out of the dining room, pushing through the door and running down the path toward the dock.

John jumped up, already heading toward the door. "The keys are in the skiff."

Together, we raced to the door and hurtled down the path toward the skiff. By the time we hit the steps down to the dock, she was already fumbling with the key in *Mooncatcher's* ignition.

"Stop!" John shouted. "There's not enough gas in the tank to get you to Mount Desert Island. And I have a direct line to the Coast Guard; they'll catch you before you get there."

"I'm not going to wait to be arrested," she spat. As she spoke, she turned the key, and the engine roared to life. John raced down the steps as she reached for the rope on the back cleat. She untied the rope, flinging it aside, and then darted to the front of the boat. John got to the dock just as she was starting to untie the second line. Instead of grabbing for the rope, though, he leapt from the dock into the boat.

"No!" she screamed. As she managed to untie the second rope, setting the skiff loose from the dock, he wrenched the key in the outboard motor, cutting the engine. She threw herself at him; for a moment, they stood, locked in a weird almost-embrace, barely balancing. Then she launched herself toward the key, which was still in the ignition. As he swiveled to keep his balance, the boat lurched, tipping them both sideways. As I watched, unable to do anything to help, they tipped over toward the dock. There was a thunk and a splash, and *Mooncatcher* drifted away from the dock, unmoored.

20

"*J*ohn!" I called. Somebody had hit the dock; was it my sweet husband?

A moment later, his head popped up. He was still holding onto Kayla, but she wasn't fighting anymore. She appeared to be limp.

"Is she okay?" I asked.

"She hit her head on the dock," he said. "Help me get her up?"

He swam her over and as he lifted her from below, I pulled her up, sliding her onto the dock. Blood and water ran down her face; her eyes were closed and her jaw slack. The tennis bracelet glinted in the morning light.

"She's breathing," I said, watching the rise and fall of her chest. I pulled my phone out of my pocket. "I'm calling 911."

John glanced back to where *Mooncatcher* was drifting away. "Do you have the keys to the *Little Marian*?" he asked, looking at my skiff, which was tied up a few feet away.

"They're in the kitchen," I said.

"If you're okay, I'll run and get them and go rescue *Mooncatcher*," he said.

The dispatcher answered as he spoke, and I nodded. "I need the police and EMT," I told the woman who had answered the phone, and as John ran back up to the inn, I watched Kayla breathing and relayed all that had happened into my phone.

Twenty minutes later, John had both skiffs tied back up and Kayla started stirring. He'd gone up and gotten blankets from the house; the water was frigid, and she was shivering in the cold wind off the water.

"You think she'll be okay?" I asked.

"I hope so," he said. He hadn't changed out of his wet clothes, refusing to leave me again until the authorities had arrived.

"Will you be?"

"All I need is a hot bath and a bowl of your potato soup," he said, grinning.

"Potato soup! Gwen! I haven't checked in with Adam in forever!"

"Why don't you text him now?" John suggested.

I grabbed my phone and pecked away at it, asking for a status update. As I waited, the phone buzzed with a response. "Definitely in labor, all is fine," I said. "The midwife is there." I looked up. "Thank goodness one thing is going right."

"You caught a murderer," John pointed out. "I think that counts as more than one thing."

"It's not all right for Justine, though," I said. "Or her family."

"You can't fix everything," he said gently. He reached out and put his chilled hand on mine. We stayed that way, holding hands as the wind whipped off the water and Kayla shivered under her blankets, until we spotted a Coast Guard cutter chugging toward dock.

"They're here," he said, standing up to wave them down.

"Thank goodness," I breathed as Kayla moaned beside me.

❧

"So, all's well that ends well," John said as I chopped up leeks and tossed them into a broth-filled pot along with peeled potatoes, chopped-up carrots, and celery. I added a pinch of salt and sat down at the table, where John had already poured me a glass of sauvignon blanc.

"Except for Justine," I said. "Mercedes' husband is pretty upset, too. He's lost both parents now."

"He's awfully young for that. Thank goodness he's got Mercedes."

"And Mercedes says they have a baby on the way themselves, so maybe that will help," I said. "She seems to have a good relationship with her parents, so at least there will be two doting grandparents on hand."

"Speaking of doting grandparents, has anyone told Bridget Gwen's in labor yet?"

I shook my head. "She asked me to wait until the baby comes. Otherwise..."

"She'd already be here," John finished for me.

"Exactly." My phone buzzed, and I looked down at the screen.

"Any word from Adam?" John asked.

"She's mostly dilated, according to my last update. They're hoping she'll start pushing and the baby will come tonight."

"If she went into labor last night, isn't this taking a long time?" he asked, a furrow of concern creasing his brow.

"I think first babies take longer," I said. "Besides, the contractions started last night, but I think she was technically not 'in labor' until this morning." John didn't look any more relaxed. "The midwife is with her," I reassured him. "And Adam will take care of her."

"He'd better," John growled. Then he looked at me. "We should probably talk about kids sometime," he said. "I mean, if we're thinking about it, we should probably address it sooner rather than later."

I swallow hard. "I guess you're right," I said. "I keep thinking things will settle down and there will be a better time, but we just keep staying busy."

"So you're thinking about it?"

"I'm not sold on the idea," I said. "But you'd be a great dad. And this is a pretty wonderful place to have a kid. The whole island would be an extended family."

"I could teach her to go fishing. Or him. And how to carve wood..." John's eyes were sparkling, and I realized with a bit of a sinking feeling that my husband did, in fact, want children of his own.

But I wasn't sure yet that I did. "I'm open to talking about it. But let's see how Gwen and Adam get on."

"If we had one soon, Gwen's kiddo and ours would grow up together," John said. "Like cousins... or even siblings."

Oh, dear. He really was on board with the idea. How had I not seen it? Maybe I did have a child in my future, I thought. "Let's wait until our niece or nephew is actually born before planning an extended family, okay?" I asked, grinning.

"Sorry," he said. "I guess... I guess I think I do want kids."

"I gathered that," I said. "Let me get used to the idea, okay? I've just had so much going on with the inn, and Gwen, and everything else..."

"I don't mean to push," he said. "Sorry. I just... with all the excitement of Gwen and Adam, I just started thinking about our own little family."

"Let's keep talking about it, okay?" I said.

"Okay," he said, leaning over and giving me a kiss. A moment later, my phone buzzed. I pulled it out and read the text.

"The baby's coming," I said. "She's pushing now."

"*I*s she okay?"

I texted quickly, and Adam responded just as fast. "She's fine... just tired."

"I can't believe Gwen is going to be a mother," John said, green eyes alight. "It'll be so amazing having a little person around. To make toys for. To watch movies with, to teach how to swim..."

"That may take a few years," I told him, grinning.

"I know, but it's fun to think about. When can we go over and visit them?"

"I think the baby has to be actually born before they want us there," I told him, laughing. As I spoke, the pot on the stove started to make bubbling noises. "In the meantime, I think the soup is boiling; let me go turn that down."

"Where's that lemon cake?" John asked.

"What's left is in the dining room," I told him. "I'll put on a pot of coffee."

"Thanks," he said, and pushed through the swinging door to the dining room.

As John and I waited, we both plowed through the rest

of the lemon cake, bite by bite. I mashed the cooked pota-toes and veggies, added milk, and then stirred together butter, flour, and herbs before mixing them into the soup, raising the heat and bringing it back to a boil before adding shredded Swiss cheese.

"That smells divine," John said as he finished off another piece of cake. How was it that he and Gwen could plow through the baked goods and still be so lean? It wasn't fair, I thought for the zillionth time as I snuck a taste of the potato cheese soup. The sweet, oniony tang of leek melded perfectly with the fresh flavor of celery and the hearty earth-iness of the pureed root vegetables, enhanced by the rich-ness of the milk and cheese. It was just the thing for a chilly spring evening.

I turned off the heat and took another sip of my milky coffee. The phone rang, and I picked it up, my heart rate picking up.

"Adam! How is she?"

"They're doing great," he said.

I looked at John. "They?"

"It's a girl!" he said. "And she's beautiful. Just under eight pounds," he said.

"I'm so glad," I said, feeling my heart swell. "When can we come and visit? I just finished making potato cheese soup."

"I'll check with Gwen and call you back," he said. "I just wanted you to be the first to know."

"Thank you," I said, feeling my heart swell with love for a little girl I hadn't even met yet.

~

TWO HOURS LATER, John, the potato cheese soup and I were at Gwen and Adam's cottage on the far side of the island. The midwife was already on her second bowl of soup, and Gwen was tucked under blankets on the sofa, looking tired but radiant. In her arms she cradled a small, perfect human being. I melted the moment I saw her.

"She's beautiful," I breathed, and the look in John's eyes told me he felt just the same way.

"We named her Eva Natalie," Gwen informed me shyly.

I blinked at her. "What?"

"You've been like a second mother to me," Gwen said. "We thought it just felt... right."

"Oh, you're going to make me cry," I told her, feeling tears well. Eva Natalie. Oh.

"Do you want to hold her?" she asked.

"I'd love to," I said, and as she handed me the soft, warm bundle, Eva's little rosebud mouth opened and closed, and her tiny, perfect hand grasped at the air. I looked into her gray-blue eyes.

"Welcome to the world, little one," I cooed, and as I touched her hand, she grasped my finger and held it.

I looked up at John, and then back at the perfect little human in my arms.

Maybe a baby wouldn't be such a bad idea, after all.

MURDER ON THE ROCKS
CHAPTER ONE

Hungry for more Maine adventures?

If you haven't explored the Gray Whale Inn mysteries yet, here's a sneak preview of the Agatha-nominated Murder on the Rocks, first in Karen's beloved ten-book (and counting) Gray Whale Inn cozy mystery series.

Chapter One

The alarm rang at 6 a.m., jolting me out from under my down comforter and into a pair of slippers. As much as I enjoyed innkeeping, I would never get used to climbing out of bed while everyone else was still sleeping. Ten minutes later I was in the kitchen, inhaling the aroma of dark-roasted coffee as I tapped it into the coffeemaker and gazing out the window at the gray-blue morning. Fog, it looked like—the swirling mist had swallowed even the Cranberry Rock lighthouse, just a quarter of a mile away. I grabbed the sugar and flour canisters from the pantry and dug a bag of blueberries out of the freezer for Wicked Blueberry Coffee Cake. The recipe was one of my favorites: not only did my guests rave over the butter-and-brown-sugar-drenched cake, but its simplicity was a drowsy cook's dream.

The coffeepot had barely finished gurgling when I sprinkled the pan of dimpled batter with brown-sugar topping and eased it into the oven. My eyes focused on the clock above the sink: 6:30. Just enough time for a relaxed thirty minutes on the kitchen porch.

Equipped with a mug of steaming French-roast coffee, I grabbed my blue windbreaker from its hook next to the door and headed out into the gray Maine morning. As hard as it was to drag myself out of a soft, warm bed while it was still dark outside, I loved mornings on Cranberry Island.

I settled myself into a white-painted wooden rocker and took a sip of strong, sweet coffee. The sound of the waves crashing against the rocks was muted, but mesmerizing. I inhaled the tangy air as I rocked, watching the fog twirl around the rocks and feeling the kiss of a breeze on my cheeks. A tern wheeled overhead as the thrum of a lobster boat rumbled across the water, pulsing and fading as it moved from trap to trap.

"Natalie!" A voice from behind me shattered my reverie. I jumped at the sound of my name, spilling coffee on my legs. "I was looking for you." Bernard Katz's bulbous nose protruded from the kitchen door. I stood up and swiped at my coffee-stained jeans. I had made it very clear that the kitchen was off-limits to guests—not only was there a sign on the door, but it was listed in the house rules guests received when they checked in.

"Can I help you with something?" I couldn't keep the anger from seeping into my voice.

"We're going to need breakfast at seven. And my son and

his wife will be joining us. She doesn't eat any fat, so you'll have to have something light for her."

"But breakfast doesn't start until 8:30."

"Yes, well, I'm sure you'll throw something together." He glanced at his watch, a Rolex the size of a life preserver. "Oops! You'd better get cracking. They'll be here in twenty minutes."

I opened my mouth to protest, but he disappeared back into my kitchen with a bang. My first impulse was to storm through the door and tell Katz he could fish for his breakfast, but my business survival instinct kicked in. Breakfast at seven? Fine. That would be an extra $50 on his bill for the extra guests—and for the inconvenience. Scrambled egg whites should do the trick for Mrs. Katz Jr. First, however, a change of clothes was in order. I swallowed what was left of my coffee and took a deep, lingering breath of the salty air before heading inside to find a fresh pair of jeans.

My stomach clenched again as I climbed the stairs to my bedroom. Bernard Katz, owner of resorts for the rich and famous, had earmarked the beautiful, and currently vacant, fifty-acre parcel of land right next to the Gray Whale Inn for his next big resort—despite the fact that the Shoreline Conservation Association had recently reached an agreement with the Cranberry Island Board of Selectmen to buy the property and protect the endangered terns that nested there. The birds had lost most of their nesting grounds to people over the past hundred years, and the small strip of beach protected by towering cliffs was home to one of the largest tern populations still in existence.

Katz, however, was keen to make sleepy little Cranberry Island the next bijou in his crown of elite resorts, and was throwing bundles of money at the board to encourage them to sell it to him instead. If Katz managed to buy the land, I was afraid the sprawling resort would mean the end not only for the terns, but for the Gray Whale Inn.

As I reached the door to my bedroom, I wondered yet again why Katz and his assistant were staying at my inn. Bernard Katz's son Stanley and his daughter-in-law Estelle owned a huge "summer cottage" called Cliffside that was just on the other side of the preserve. I had been tempted to decline Katz's reservation, but the state of my financial affairs made it impossible to refuse any request for a week in two of my most expensive rooms.

I reminded myself that while Katz and his assistant Ogden Wilson were odious, my other guests—the Bittles, a retired couple up from Alabama for an artists' retreat—were lovely, and deserved a wonderful vacation. And at least Katz had paid up front. As of last Friday, my checking account had dropped to under $300, and the next mortgage payment was due in two weeks. Although Katz's arrival on the island might mean the eventual end of the Gray Whale Inn, right now I needed the cash.

Goosebumps crept up my legs under the wet denim as I searched for something to wear. Despite the fact that it was June, and one of the warmer months of the year, my body hadn't adjusted to Maine's lower temperatures. I had spent the last fifteen years under Austin's searing sun, working for the Texas Department of Parks and Wildlife and dreaming of someday moving to the coast to start a bed-and-breakfast.

I had discovered the Gray Whale Inn while staying with a friend in a house she rented every summer on Mount Desert Island. I had come to Maine to heal a broken heart, and had no idea I'd fall in love all over again—this time with a 150-year-old former sea captain's house on a small island accessible only by boat.

The inn was magical; light airy rooms with views of the

sea, acres of beach roses, and sweet peas climbing across the balconies. I jotted down the real estate agent's number and called on a whim, never guessing that my long-term fantasy might be within my grasp. When the agent informed me that the inn was for sale at a bargain price, I raced to put together enough money for a down payment.

I had had the good fortune to buy a large old house when Austin was a sleepy town in a slump. After a room-by-room renovation, it sold for three times the original price, and between the proceeds of the house and my entire retirement savings, there was just enough money to take out a mortgage on the inn. A mortgage, I reflected as I strained to button my last pair of clean jeans, whose monthly payments were equivalent to the annual Gross National Product of Sweden.

I tossed my coffee-stained jeans into the overflowing laundry basket and paused for a last-minute inspection in the cloudy mirror above the dresser. Gray eyes looked back at me from a face only slightly plump from two months of butter-and sugar-laden breakfasts and cookies. I took a few swipes at my bobbed brown hair with a brush and checked for white hairs—no new ones today, although with the Katzes around my hair might be solid white by the end of the summer. If I hadn't already torn all of my hair out, that is.

When I pushed through the swinging door to the dining room at 7:00, Bernard Katz sat alone, gazing out the broad sweep of windows toward the section of coastline he had earmarked for his golf course. He looked like a banker in a blue pinstriped three-piece suit whose buttons strained to cover his round stomach. Katz turned at the sound of my footsteps, exposing a line of crooked teeth as he smiled. He was a self-made man, someone had told me. Apparently there'd been no money in the family budget for orthodontic work. Still, if I had enough money to buy islands, I'd have found a couple of thousand dollars to spare for straight teeth.

"Coffee. Perfect." He plucked the heavy blue mug from the place setting in front of him and held it out. "I'll take cream and sugar." I filled his cup, congratulating myself for not spilling it on his pants, then plunked the cream pitcher and sugar bowl on the table.

"You know, you stand to earn quite a bit of business from our little project." Katz took a sip of coffee. "Not bad," he said, sounding surprised. "Anyway, there's always a bit of overflow in the busy season. We might be able to arrange something so that your guests could use our facilities. For a fee, of course."

Of course. He leaned back and put his expensively loafered feet on one of my chairs. Apparently he was willing to cough up some change for footwear. "I know starting a business is tough, and it looks like your occupancy is on the low side." He nodded at the room full of empty tables.

"Well, it is an hour and a half before breakfast." He didn't have to know that only two other rooms were booked —and one of those was for Barbara Eggleby, the Shoreline Conservation Association representative who was coming to the island for the sole purpose of preventing his development from happening.

"Still," he went on, "this is the high season." His eyes swept over the empty tables. "Or should be. Most of the inns in this area are booked to capacity." My first impulse was to respond that most of the inns in the area had been open for more than two months, and that he was welcome to go to the mainland and stay at one of them, but I held my tongue.

He removed his feet from my chair and leaned toward

me. "Our resort will make Cranberry Island *the* hot spot for the rich and famous in Maine. Kennebunkport won't know what hit it. Your place will be perfect for the people who want glitz but can't afford the price tag of the resort."

Glitz? The whole point of Cranberry Island was its ruggedness and natural beauty. So my inn would be a catchall for poor people who couldn't quite swing the gigantic tab at Katz's mega resort. Lovely.

I smiled. "Actually, I think the island works better as a place to get away from all the 'glitz'. And I don't think a golf course would do much to enhance the island's appeal." I paused for a moment. "Or the nesting success of the black-chinned terns."

"Oh, yes, the birds." He tsked and shook his head. The sun gleamed on his bald pate, highlighting the liver spots that had begun to appear like oversized freckles. "I almost forgot, you're heading up that greenie committee. I would have thought you were smarter than that, being a business-woman." He waved a hand. "Well, I'm sure we could work something out, you know, move the nests somewhere else or something."

"Good morning, Bernie." The sharp report of stiletto heels rescued me from having to respond. *Bernie?*

"Estelle!" Katz virtually leaped from his chair. "Please, sit down." Katz's daughter-in-law approached the table in a blaze of fuchsia and decorated Katz's cheeks with two air kisses before favoring him with a brilliant smile of straight, pearl-white teeth. Clearly orthodontic work had been a priority for her. Her frosted blonde hair was coiffed in a Marilyn Monroe pouf, and the neckline of her hot pink suit plunged low enough to expose a touch of black lace bra. An interesting choice for a foggy island morning on the coast of Maine. Maybe this was what Katz meant by glitz.

She turned her ice-blue eyes to me and arranged her frosted pink lips in a hard line. "Coffee. Black." She returned her gaze to Katz, composing her face into a simpering smile as he pulled out a chair for her.

"Estelle, I'm so glad you could come. Where's Stanley?" Stanley Katz was Bernard Katz's son, and Estelle's husband. I'd seen him around the island; he had inherited his father's girth and balding pate, but not his business sense or charisma. Stanley and Estelle had seemed like a mismatched couple to me until I found out the Katzes were rolling in the green stuff. As much as I didn't like the Katzes, I felt sorry for Stanley. Between his overbearing father and his glamorous wife, he faded into the background.

"Stanley?" Estelle looked like she was searching her brain to place the name. "Oh, he's out parking the car. I didn't want to have to walk over all of those horrid rocks." She fixed me with a stare. "You really should build a proper walkway. I could have broken a heel."

Katz chuckled. "When the Cranberry Island Premier Resort is built, you won't have to worry about any rocks, my dear." Or birds, or plants, or anything else that was "inconvenient." Their voices floated over my shoulder as I headed back to the kitchen. "You look stunning as usual, Estelle."

"Keep saying things like that and I'll be wishing I'd married *you*!" I rolled my eyes as the kitchen door swung shut behind me. The aroma of coffee cake enveloped me as I ran down my mental checklist. Fruit salad, whole wheat toast, and skinny scrambled eggs for Estelle; scrambled whole eggs and blueberry coffee cake would work for Katz, who from the bulge over his pin-striped pants didn't seem too interested in Weight Watchers-style breakfasts. I tugged at the snug waistband of my jeans and grimaced. At least Katz and I had one thing in common. I grabbed a crystal bowl from the cabinet and two melons from the countertop.

As the French chef's knife sliced through the orange flesh of a cantaloupe, my eyes drifted to the window. I hoped the blanket of fog would lift soon. The Cranberry Island Board of Selectmen was meeting tonight to decide what to do with the land next door, and Barbara Eggleby, the Shoreline Conservation Association representative, was due in today. I was afraid the bad weather might delay her flight. *Save Our Terns*, the three-person island group I had formed to save the terns' nesting ground from development, was counting on Barbara for the financial backing to combat Katz's bid for development. As I slid melon chunks into the bowl and retrieved a box of berries from the refrigerator, my eyes returned to the window. The fog did look like it was letting up a bit. I could make out a lobster boat chugging across the leaden water. The berries tumbled into a silver colander like dark blue and red gems, and as the water from the faucet gushed over them, the small boat paused to haul a trap. A moment later, the engine growled as the boat turned and steamed toward the mainland, threading its way through the myriad of brightly colored buoys that studded the cold saltwater.

Since moving to the island, I had learned that each lobsterman had a signature buoy color that enabled him to recognize his own traps, as well as the traps of others. I had been surprised to discover that what I thought of as open ocean was actually carved up into unofficial but zealously guarded fishing territories.

My eyes followed the receding boat as I gave the berries a final swirl and turned off the faucet. Lately, some of the lobstermen from the mainland had been encroaching on island territory, and the local lobster co-op was in an uproar.

I strained my eyes to see if any of the offending red and green buoys were present. The veil of fog thinned for a moment, and sure enough, bobbing next to a jaunty pink and white one was a trio of what looked like nautical Christmas ornaments.

The boat had vanished from sight by the time the fruit salad was finished. I eyed my creation—the blueberries and raspberries interspersed with the bright green of kiwi made a perfect complement to the cantaloupe—and opened the fridge to retrieve a dozen eggs and some fat-free milk. When I turned around, I slammed into Ogden Wilson, Katz's skinny assistant. My fingers tightened on the milk before it could slip from my grasp, but the impact jolted the eggs out of my hand. I stifled a curse as the carton hit the floor. Was I going to have to install a lock on the kitchen door?

Ogden didn't apologize. Nor did he stoop to help me collect the egg carton, which was upended in a gelatinous mess on my hardwood floor. "Mr. Katz would like to know when breakfast will be ready." His eyes bulged behind the thick lenses of his glasses. With his oily pale skin and lanky body, he reminded me of some kind of cave-dwelling amphibian. I wished he'd crawl back into his hole.

I bent down to inventory the carton; only three of the dozen had survived. "Well, now that we're out of eggs, it will be a few minutes later." It occurred to me that I hadn't considered him when doing the breakfast tally. Although Ogden generally stuck to his boss like glue, it was easy to forget he existed. "Are you going to be joining them?"

"Of course. But do try to hurry. Mr. Katz has an extremely busy schedule."

"Well, I'm afraid breakfast will be slightly delayed." I tipped my chin toward the mess on the floor. "But I'll see what I can do."

The oven timer buzzed as Ogden slipped through the swinging door to the dining room. I rescued the cake from the oven and squatted to clean up the mess on the floor. What kind of urgent business could Bernard Katz have on an island of less than a square mile? Most of the movers and shakers here were fishermen's wives after a few too many beers. I hoped Barbara Eggleby would be able to convince the board that the Shoreline Conservation Association was the right choice for the land next door. The Katz development would be a cancer on the island. Lord knew the Katzes were.

I raced up the stairs and knocked on my niece's door. Gwen had come to work with me for the summer, cleaning the rooms, covering the phones, and helping with the cooking from time to time in exchange for room and board. The help was a godsend— not only was it free, but it allowed me time to work on promoting the inn—but Gwen was not a perfect assistant.

Part of the reason Gwen was spending the summer at the inn was that her mother didn't know what else to do with her: she'd flunked half of her classes her first year at UCLA and my sister couldn't spend more than ten minutes in the same room with her daughter without one or the other of them declaring war. Her work at the inn, while not F-level, was between a B and a C, when I needed everything to be A+. Still, help was help, and beggars couldn't be choosers. I wished that some of the enthusiasm she showed for the art classes she was taking on the island would spill over to her housekeeping skills.

"Who is it?" answered a groggy voice from the other side of the door. I cracked the door open. Gwen's hair was a messy brown halo in the dim light from the curtained window.

"I'm sorry to wake you, but I need you to run down to Charlene's and get a dozen eggs."

"What time is it?"

"It's just after seven. Please hurry... I've got guests waiting."

She groaned. "Seven in the *morning*?"

"I know. But it's an emergency." She grumbled something and began to move toward the side of the bed, so I closed the door and jogged back down the stairs. I'd start with fruit salad and a plate of coffee cake, and bring out the eggs later. Maybe a pan of sausage, too... I could keep it warm until the Bittles came down at 8:30.

I was retrieving a package of pork sausages from the freezer when someone tapped on the door to the back porch. I whirled around to tell the Katzes I'd meet them in the dining room shortly, and saw the sun-streaked brown hair of my neighbor, John Quinton. "Come in!" I hollered, smiling for the first time that morning.

John's green eyes twinkled in a face already brown from afternoons out on the water in his sailboat, and his faded green T-shirt and shorts were streaked with sawdust. John was both a friend and a tenant; he rented the inn's converted carriage house from me, as well as a small shed he had converted to a workshop. He was a sculptor who created beautiful things from the driftwood that washed up on the beaches, but supplemented what he called his "art habit" with a variety of part-time jobs. In the spring and summer, he made toy sailboats for the gift shop on the pier. He also held a year-round job as the island's only deputy.

"You're up early. Working on a new project?" I asked.

"Island Artists ordered a few more boats. I figured I'd churn them out this morning and then start on some fun stuff." His eyes glinted with mischief. "One of Claudette's goats was eyeing your sweet peas, by the way. I shooed her off, but I'm afraid she'll be back."

I groaned. Claudette White was one of the three members of *Save Our Terns*, and was known on the island as "eccentric." Although her husband, Eleazer, was a boat-builder and popular with the locals, most of the islanders gave Claudette a wide berth. Her goats were almost as unpopular as she was, since they were notorious for escaping and consuming other people's gardens.

When Claudette wasn't caring for her goats or knitting their wool into sweaters and hats, she was holding forth at length about the evils of the modern world to anyone who would listen. I wasn't delighted that she had chosen to join *Save Our Terns*, but since the only other takers had been my best friend, Charlene, and me, we didn't feel we could turn her down.

John watched me pry sausage links out of a box and into a cast-iron pan. "I'm not the only one up early. I thought breakfast wasn't till 8:30."

"Yeah, well, we're working on Katz time today." A thump came from overhead, and then the sound of the shower. I sighed: so much for urgency. Gwen must be performing her morning ablutions. I appealed to John for help. "Do you have any eggs I can borrow? I was going to send Gwen down to the store, but I'm short on time."

"I just picked up a dozen yesterday. Is that enough?"

"You're a lifesaver." He disappeared through the back door, and the thought flitted through my mind that he might stay for a cup of coffee when he got back. I spooned fruit salad into a crystal bowl and reminded myself that John had a girlfriend in Portland. Five minutes later I sailed into the dining room bearing the fruit salad and a platter mounded with hot coffee cake. Stanley Katz had arrived, and sat hunched in an ill-fitting brown suit next to his wife. Estelle glared at me. "Coffee cake? I can't eat that. I thought this breakfast was supposed to be low-fat!" Then she pointed a lacquered nail at the ginger-colored cat who had curled up in a sunbeam on the windowsill. "And why is there a *cat* in your dining room? Surely that's against health department regulations?"

I scooped up Biscuit and deposited her in the living room. She narrowed her gold-green eyes at me and stalked over to the sofa as I hurried back into the dining room. "I'll have skinny scrambled eggs and wheat toast out shortly," I said. "We had a slight mishap in the kitchen." I shot Ogden a look. He blinked behind his thick lenses. I attempted a bright smile. "Can I get anybody more coffee?"

Estelle sighed. "I suppose so." She turned to her father-in-law, who had already transferred two pieces of cake to his plate. "With this kind of service," she muttered under her breath, "I don't know how she expects to stay in business."

When I got back into the kitchen, a carton of eggs lay on the butcher-block counter. Darn. I'd missed John. The sausages had started to sizzle and Estelle's egg whites were almost done when the phone rang.

"Nat."

"Charlene? You're up early." Charlene was the local grocer, a fellow member of *Save Our Terns*, and my source for island gossip. She was also my best friend.

"I've got bad news."

I groaned. "You're kidding. The Katzes sprang a surprise 7 a.m. breakfast on me and then his assistant broke all of my eggs. It can't get any worse."

"It can. I just talked to the coastal airport: no planes in or out, probably for the whole day. A big nor'easter is about to hit the coast."

My heart thumped in my chest. "The airport is closed? So Barbara isn't going to make it in time for the council meeting?"

"It's just you and me, babe. And Claudette."

My stomach sank. Without a representative from the Shoreline Conservation Association to combat Katz's offer for the property next to the inn, we could only sit and watch as Katz wooed the board of selectmen with visions of the fat bank accounts the island would enjoy when the Cranberry Island Premier Resort came into being.

I leaned my head against the wall. "We're sunk."

Download your copy of Murder on the Rocks now to find out what happens next!

Praise for the Gray Whale Inn mysteries...

"This book is an absolute gem." — Suspense Magazine

"Deliciously clever plot. Juicy characters. Karen MacInerney has cooked up a winning recipe for murder. **Don't miss this mystery!**" — *New York Times* Bestselling Author Maggie Sefton

"...a new **cozy author worth investigating.**" — Publishers Weekly

"Murder on the Rocks mixes a pinch of salt air, a hunky love interest, an island divided by environmental issues... and, of course, murder. **Add Karen MacInerney to your list of favorite Maine mystery authors.**" — Lea Wait, author of the Antique Print mystery series

"Sure to please cozy readers." — Library Journal

"I look anxiously forward to the sequel... Karen MacInerney has a **winning recipe for a great series.**" — Julie Obermiller, Features Editor, Mysterical-E

MORE BOOKS BY KAREN MACINERNEY

To download a free book and receive members-only outtakes, giveaways, short stories, recipes, and updates, join Karen's Reader's Circle at www.karenmaciner ney.com! You can also join her Facebook community; she often hosts giveaways and loves getting to know her readers there.

And don't forget to follow her on BookBub to get newsflashes on new releases!

The Snug Harbor Mysteries
A Killer Ending
Inked Out
The Lies that Bind
Snug Harbor Cozy Mystery #4 (Coming 2023)

The Gray Whale Inn Mysteries
Murder on the Rocks
Dead and Berried
Murder Most Maine

Berried to the Hilt
Brush With Death
Death Runs Adrift
Whale of a Crime
Claws for Alarm
Scone Cold Dead
Anchored Inn
Gray Whale Inn Mystery #11 (Coming 2023)
Cookbook: The Gray Whale Inn Kitchen
Four Seasons of Mystery (A Gray Whale Inn Collection)
Blueberry Blues (A Gray Whale Inn Short Story)
Pumpkin Pied (A Gray Whale Inn Short Story)
Iced Inn (A Gray Whale Inn Short Story)
Lupine Lies (A Gray Whale Inn Short Story)

The Dewberry Farm Mysteries

Killer Jam
Fatal Frost
Deadly Brew
Mistletoe Murder
Dyeing Season
Wicked Harvest
Sweet Revenge
Peach Clobber
Dewberry Farm Mystery #9 (Coming 2023)
Slay Bells Ring: A Dewberry Farm Christmas Story
Cookbook: Lucy's Farmhouse Kitchen

The Margie Peterson Mysteries

Mother's Day Out
Mother Knows Best
Mother's Little Helper

Wolves and the City
   Howling at the Moon
   On the Prowl
   Leader of the Pack

RECIPES

LEMON SUNSHINE BUNDT CAKE

Ingredients

Bundt Cake

- 1 cup butter, softened to room temperature
- 2 cups granulated sugar
- 2 Tbsp lemon zest
- 4 eggs, large
- 3/4 tsp salt
- 2 tsp baking powder
- 2 3/4 cup all purpose flour
- 3 Tbsp cornstarch
- 1/2 cup milk
- 1/4 cup fresh lemon juice
- 1/4 cup sour cream
- 1 tsp vanilla extract

Lemon Icing

- 1 1/2 cups powdered sugar
- 2-3 Tbsp lemon juice
- 1 tsp lemon zest

Instructions

Lemon Bundt Cake

1. Preheat oven to 350 degrees.
2. Cream the butter until light and fluffy.
3. Add sugar and lemon zest to the butter, mixing until it is well combined.
4. Add in the eggs, one at a time, beating well after each addition.
5. In a second bowl, whisk together salt, baking powder, flour and cornstarch. Set aside.
6. In a third bowl, mix together lemon juice, milk and vanilla extract.
7. Add the flour mixture and milk mixture to the butter mixture, alternating dry and wet ingredients and beginning and ending with the flour. Mix until everything is just combined.
8. Add in sour cream and mix until just combined.
9. Grease your Bundt cake pan well and pour the batter evenly into the pan.
10. Bake for 45-55 minutes, or until a toothpick comes out clean.
11. Allow to cool for about 10-15 minutes, then remove the cake from the Bundt pan and allow it to finish cooling on a wire rack or plate.

Lemon Icing

1. Whisk powdered sugar, lemon juice and lemon zest together. Once combined, drizzle over the cooled cake. Allow the icing to set about 5 minutes before serving.

POTATO CHEESE SOUP

Ingredients

- 4 potatoes, peeled and quartered
- 1 small carrot, finely chopped
- ½ stalk celery, finely chopped
- White part of 3 large leeks, minced
- 1 ½ cups chicken broth
- 1 teaspoon salt
- 2 ½ cups milk
- 3 tablespoons butter, melted
- 3 tablespoons all-purpose flour
- 3 tablespoons minced fresh or 1 tablespoon dried parsley
- 1 teaspoon ground black pepper
- 1 cup shredded Swiss cheese (plus more to garnish)
- Chopped bacon to garnish (optional)

Instructions

1. In a large saucepan, bring potatoes, carrots, celery, leeks, chicken broth and salt to a boil. Reduce heat; cover and simmer until potatoes are just tender. Do not rinse: mash mixture slightly. Stir in milk.

2. In a small mixing bowl, blend butter, flour, parsley, and pepper; stir into potato mixture. Cook and stir over medium heat until thickened and bubbly.

3. Remove from heat: add cheese and stir until cheese is almost melted. Serve in individual bowls sprinkled with extra shredded cheese and chopped bacon.

MARGUČIAI (EGG DECORATING) INSTRUCTIONS

How to make Marguciai

In Lithuania, there are two methods for decorating eggs; you can decorate blown eggs, like Agnes does in BASKET CASE, or simply decorate hard-boiled eggs for Easter use. My grandmother, whose maiden name actually was Agnes Masaitis, was a first-generation American whose parents were born in Lithuania. Unfortunately, while I have fond memories of dyeing Easter eggs at her Pennsylvania home in my blue-checked pajamas and then eating coconut-covered Easter "lamb", she never did teach me how to make Marguciai, perhaps because her own mother died when she was still young. So I researched the craft myself, in part to remember my sweet grandmother, who also had the BEST maple twists waiting for me when I visited, taught me how to use a wringer washer (which still scares the dickens out of me), and always made me root beer floats to drink after catching fireflies in mason jars.

Now, for how to decorate the eggs. The "scratch method" is based on producing designs on dyed eggs by scratching or carving the surface of the shell. This is a simple method, requiring very simple tools - any sharp, pointy tool can work, such as an Exacto knife or a paring knife. . Short, straight, and white scratch lines are the basic elements of design for this method, but the results can be absolutely stunning.

Wax patterning is second method commonly used by Lithuanians for decorating eggs. Beeswax is used, not paraffin: it can be melted in a tealight holder and kept hot and ready for use. The hot wax is then applied in patterns with a round-headed pin embedded in a pencil eraser. The basic elements for creating decorative designs with this method are dots and "tailed" dots. A dot is produced by dipping the tip of your pin into hot wax and setting it momentarily on the egg's surface, then lifting. A "tailed" dot results when the tool is moved on the egg's surface before lifting.

After creating the pattern, the egg is dyed in a solution that is cooler than the melting temperature of the wax. After dyeing, the wax is removed by heating the egg in an oven or rolling it on a hot towel. The removed wax reveals a white pattern. To create a multi-colored pattern, repeat cycles of wax application and dyeing.

The typical dyes sold in stores work just fine for these eggs, or you can use natural dyes from recipes available online. (Apparently Lithuanian tradition involves making them shiny by rubbing the eggs with pork fat and then polishing them with a cloth, but I've never tried it myself.) You can search for design examples to inspire you online, but below is a list of common colors and meanings.

Happy decorating!

Symbolism of Colors
Red (Raudona) - Beauty, love, passion, enthusiasm
Orange (Oranzinai)- Endurance, strength, power
Yellow (Geltona) - Spirituality, youth, light, purity, happiness, wisdom
Green (Zalia) - Youth, growing, renewal, freshness, hope
Blue (Melyna) - Endurance, strength, power
Purple (Purpurine) - Patience, power, royalty
Black (Juoda) - Eternity and death
White (Balta) - Purity, birth, virginity, and ignorance
Brown (Ruda) - Earth

Symbolism of Designs
Deer - Wealth/ Prosperity
Leaves & Flowers - Life/Growth
Circles - Protection and everlasting life, continuity, and completeness, as well as the sun.
Sun - The life-giving, all-embracing, all-renewing nature of God.
Stars & Roses - Purity, life, the giver of light, divine will of God, and God's love for humanity.
Wheat - Bountiful Harvest.
Plant Symbols - Stand for rebirth and nature
Leaves - Immortality, eternal or pure love, strength and persistence
Flowers - Beauty and Children
The 8- Point Star - Ancient symbol of Jesus Christ

Dots or Small Circles - Mary's Tears or the sun

Spirals - The mystery of life and death, as well as divinity and immortality

Cross - Jesus's Crucifixion

ABOUT THE AUTHOR

Karen is the housework-impaired, award-winning author of multiple mystery series, and her victims number well into the double digits. She lives in Georgetown, Texas with her sassy family, Tristan, and Little Bit (a.k.a. Dog #1 and Dog #2).

Feel free to visit Karen's web site, where you can download a free book and sign up for her Readers' Circle to receive subscriber-only short stories, deleted scenes, recipes and other bonus material. You can also find her on Facebook (she spends an inordinate amount of time there), where Karen loves getting to know her readers, answering questions, and offering quirky, behind-the-scenes looks at the writing process (and life in general). And please follow her on Bookbub to find out about new releases and sales!

P. S. Don't forget to follow Karen on BookBub to get newsflashes on new releases!

www.karenmacinerney.com
karen@karenmacinerney.com

facebook.com/AuthorKarenMacInerney
twitter.com/KarenMacInerney

Made in the USA
Middletown, DE
07 April 2023